Grace Upon Grace

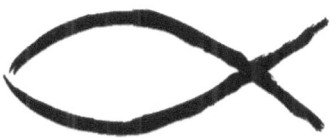

Grace Upon Grace

SEQUEL TO
SLAVE TO GRACE

JOYCE FOX

DocUmeant Publishing
85 N. Main Street
Florida, NY 10921

646-233-4366

Disclaimer: All characters except those named in the book of Philemon have been named after authentic Christian martyrs listed either in Foxe's Book of Martyr's or other martyr lists.

Scripture quotations are taken from the Holy Bible, New Living Translation, copyright ©1996, 2004, 2007 by Tyndale House Foundation. Used by permission of Tyndale House Publishers, Inc., Carol Stream, Illinois 60188. All rights reserved.

Ginger Marks Cover design and Layout
DocUmeantDesigns, www.DocUmeantDesigns.com

Philip S Marks Editor

Distributed by DocUmeant Publishing

For inquiries about volume orders, please contact:
DocUmeant Publishing
publisher@documeantpublishing.com

Printed in the United States Of America
ISBN-13: 978-1-950075-31-7

To Sgt. Ruthey Forgey: You found a way to relight the fire, and I thank you.

PROLOGUE

O nesimus! It's Onesimus! He's come back!" Petros, a full foot taller than when Onesimus ran away, jumped toward the door his now cracking voice calling, "Father! Onesimus is . . ."

Philemon appeared behind the boy and crossed rapidly toward the door. Onesimus almost took to his heels as he saw his former master bearing down on him, but he stood his ground even when Philemon reached roughly for him. The all-engulfing hug his master bestowed upon him was not what he had expected at all, but it didn't take long for him to return the hug.

Philemon pulled away and the runaway was startled to see tears in the man's eyes. "Onesimus, my son! For so long we have watched for you. I have much to tell you and," he dropped his eyes to his feet and then looked up again, "an apology to give you! Do you remember that just before you . . . left . . . Petros came in and insisted that I go with him to his grandfather's cottage because he had something to show me?"

Onesimus thought back to that day and then nodded. He and Philemon found seats on the portico.

"It was with great joy that I returned to the press room after that little trek. I was ready to tell you that all was well. Petros had found out that his grandfather, struck by the moon as he was, had taken the two missing amphorae of oil from one of the wagons because he felt he would need that much to bathe in so that he could slip from the grasp of the Angel of Death! And then we found you gone." This last was said quietly with great sorrow.

"I am so sorry I accused you Onesimus, and I am sorry that I was not a better Christian in your presence. Even being with me every day for four months you were afraid for your life! No slave should ever have to fear for their lives when their master is a follower of Christ!"

Philemon fell silent and Onesimus swallowed a large lump that had grown in his throat.

"I, too, have an apology, Master. I should never have assumed the worst of you. I knew you were a kind and just man and I did you a grave injustice when I stole your money and ran away. My sorrow for what I have done to you is unbearable and how I have ruined my own reputation would be agonizing except that I can see, in all of this, the very hand of Yahweh at work in my life."

Philemon raised startled eyes to Onesimus and tipped his head to the left.

"Your life and teachings did much to help me understand your religion, but while I was on my . . . flight . . . I met a man who slowly introduced me personally to the God of Israel. I stayed with him and learned from him for many months, knowing from the first that I would need to come back and make things right with you. At long last, he gave me a letter to give to you and told me to tell you he has plans to come to you shortly. Here it is!" He handed the letter over to Philemon and smiled when his master saw from whom the letter came.

"Paulus? You lived with Paulus and learned from him? How wonderful!" He exclaimed. "And he is coming here? Do you know when? How is he? Is he well? We heard that he was under house arrest for a while. Can you . . ."

Onesimus smiled and answered all the questions he could about Paulus's state of health and all he knew about Paulus's plans to visit Colossae, until finally, everything seemed to have been said. They had talked through the afternoon and the sun was heading toward its bed. The mourning doves were roosting in the nearby trees and their quiet cooing uttered peace to the weary souls.

"Father," Blandina called from inside the house. "Supper is almost ready."

"Oh! My! It's late, Onesimus! And no work has been done this live-long day," Philemon said. "Too late to start clerking for me right now, so why don't you go back to the slaves' quarters and tell them I want you to settle in? Supper will be served there shortly and I'm sure they've heard that you're back with us. Justin will have made arrangements for you and . . . I expect to see you bright and early tomorrow. We have much to do to prepare for the harvest!"

"Yes, sir! Bright and early!" Onesimus replied. "Bright and early!"

CHAPTER ONE

Onesimus stood outside the doorway and listened to his fellow-slaves as they began to seat themselves around the table. Chatter about events of the day and laughter concerning a small mistake one of the field hands had made sounded so warm and welcoming. He breathed deeply, smelling the fresh bread, and hurried to step inside.

The sound of his sandals on the wooden floor diverted the attention of the room's occupants to the doorway. The talk faded away, the laughter was silenced, and all was still as the diners recognized their former associate and sat wondering how to react to the presence of this runaway thief who had had the audacity to return.

"Hello," Onesimus said simply. He had no idea what he should say next. He certainly didn't want to seem to be justifying his flight or his return, but he also didn't want to leave everyone wondering what had happened. Instead, he continued, "I'm back. The Master and I've talked, and he has forgiven me. Will you? May I join you?"

It looked at first as if Onesimus would end up sitting by himself until Vitus jumped up and ran up to him. "Onesimus! I'm so glad you're back! The Master was so upset when you left I thought he would never smile again."

Justin stood up and threw his arm around Onesimus' shoulder. "It was really bad around here for a while after you left. The Master was so sad and worried. The only thing that kept him strong was his faith in Yeshua. I, too, am glad you're back, Onesimus. Come sit by me and you can tell us all about your adventures over the next few days."

Apollonia, who had lain awake nights for months after Onesimus's disappearance, just stood and watched silently as Onesimus seated himself and reached for the hands of his fellow-slaves for the dinner-time prayer. What he did next surprised almost everyone present. Only those who had been able to witness the homecoming personally knew that Onesimus had spent time with Paulus and carried his commendation.

As Justin cleared his throat to begin the prayer, Onesimus spoke up. "Justin, would you mind if I led prayer tonight?"

At Justin's nod, Onesimus began, "Loving Heavenly Father, in humility and trust we come to You to offer You our gratitude and worship. As we bow with open hearts, we ask that You bless our meal together and bless those who worked so hard to prepare it for us. Keep us in Your protection and help us to serve our Master just as we would serve You . . . with all our hearts, our minds, and our might. In the Holy name of Yeshua, Amen."

As Onesimus glanced up he saw Apollonia at the other end of the table and she was not smiling. In fact, she was frowning mightily. Puzzled, Onesimus turned his attention to the food as he determined to talk with her as soon as the meal was done.

The tables were cleared and had been re-set with basins and amphorae of water for the morning wash up. The women were leaving the men's quarters for the night as Apollonia walked past Onesimus without acknowledging his presence and headed toward the door. "Apollonia!" he called as she went by.

Apollonia turned and Onesimus saw she was still frowning.

"Let me walk outside with you," he said, and she nodded her assent.

It only took three steps before the young woman turned to face him.

"Who do you think you are? Have you any idea how much you put the Master through? How worried and broken hearted we . . . he was? And then to come strolling back and expect to take up exactly where you left off is just . . . just . . . and don't think that flowery prayer you prayed at the meal impressed me one bit! I know you well enough to know you have the most charming, most devastatingly sincere way of pretense! I don't wish to talk with you, I don't want to hear your pretty explanations, I don't want to be anywhere *near* you!" She lifted her hand and slapped him, hard, across the cheek and then turned and ran to the women's quarters.

Onesimus stood there, hand to his stinging cheek, and watched her until she entered her quarters. Then, shoulders slumped, he turned and went back into the men's quarters where he was welcomed and shunned, smiled at and glared at, and spoken to and ignored, according to each of his fellow servants' opinion.

"Your couch is still empty and your things are still in your cupboard," Justin said heartily. "Could you tell a little of your adventure before we retire?"

Vitus came up, "Yes. Do tell us why you ran! What happened to you on the road? Where did you go and who did you see?"

The rest of the gathering was obviously making decisions about whether to join the group and learn of the former runaway's odyssey or whether to continue to shun him and make him pay for his perfidy. Some chose the latter, but most allowed their curiosity to sway their emotions and came to join the group gathered around the table.

Onesimus had thought long and hard about what he should reveal and what he should keep to himself on his journey home because he knew this curiosity would be a big part of his homecoming. Praying along the way had helped him come to the conclusion that if he were to satisfy the curious, he'd better do so by telling the whole truth. Truth, according to Yeshua, was the means to be set free and Onesimus hoped that truth, told carefully and without embellishment, would be the means used to free some of his fellow slaves from disbelief.

"I ran because I was afraid," he began, and the room grew still.

"I was sold into slavery by my father to pay off his debts and I knew how our family had treated slaves who pilfered things. My trust in others had been shattered when my father proved to me that betrayal could come from the most trusted of family members and I felt I could trust no one... not even a normally kind Master.

"Then the Master called me out of the olive press and told me he had found that there were two amphorae of olive oil missing. He told me that if I had done this thing he understood that I may have needed something but that I should have come to him rather than taking the oil to sell.

"I had not taken the oil and I asked for time to find the discrepancy and he gave me that but at the end of three days of searching the records I still could not find those two amphorae. And all I could think of was

how my family would have treated a slave suspected of such treachery
. . . and I was afraid that the Master would do to me what I would have
done in his place. So I took the first opportunity, when little master
came into the olive press and insisted that Master go with him, and
I stole a purse full of gold coins and ran, heading toward Ephesus and
Rome where I hoped to get lost in the crowds of the city."

Onesimus continued to tell his tale, telling of his trip through the
fields and forests, recounting how he avoided walking on the road for
fear of discovery. He told of coming to the small village and witnessing
the branding of a runaway slave the people had caught and how that
incident strengthened his desire to hide and run. He told of his disap-
pointment when he found he had missed the last boat to sail for the
season and his worry about where he could find lodging to await the
spring and his chance to continue his flight. He ended his night's tale
with his wandering through the city of Ephesus and considering whether
to winter there or set out overland for Rome.

"And that, my friends, is the beginning of my journey that ended
today as I became a slave who is free in the only way that matters.

"We can talk more tomorrow but I'm very tired and I'm looking
forward to my couch! Goodnight."

With that he rose amid the groans of those who wished to hear
more. Did he winter in the city or did he travel overland to Rome?
How did he survive? Questions flew at him, but Onesimus, being a
consummate story-teller refused to say another word knowing that their
curiosity would bring them back for more the next night and, in time,
he could tell of his conversion and his return to Philemon's household
in such a way that those fellow-slaves who still did not believe would get
one more chance to bow before the King of Kings.

αω

CHAPTER TWO

O nesimus spent the next day acquainting himself with all the financial dealings that had gone on in his absence.

Philemon had taken back the duties of bookkeeper after he disappeared and so there was no problem with understanding what had transpired. It was simply a matter of seeing the records for the past harvests and comprehending the income and outgo for the business.

There had been no new slaves added to the household and everyone still maintained the same positions they had had before he left so he was familiar with everyone there.

He found out that Philemon's moon-mad father who had tried to oil himself up to slip out of the grasp of Death had found peace and was now lying at rest in a nearby tomb. He also discovered that Quintin was beginning to discover girls and Blandina had slimmed down and was wearing her hair up on her head and walking like a lady instead of running across wheat fields shouting at the top of her lungs. It made him slightly sad to realize how much change the children had undergone and how much he had missed.

Archippus followed his brother Justin's lead and accepted Onesimus back into the group but Barsabas was struggling with his feelings of anger toward his fellow-slave although he was trying to be neutral even when he couldn't bring himself to be friendly. Onesimus did understand and tried not to let it bother him. Whenever Barsabas turned his back and couldn't bring himself to speak, Onesimus just breathed a short prayer and went on his way.

A few of his fellow-slaves told him they had cheered him on when he ran and thought he should have stayed in Rome. To these, he explained gently that since he had found peace through the grace of Yeshua, he could not remain a runaway but had to return to the master who had treated him with kindness both before he left and after he returned.

Apollonia refused to speak to him or even to look at him as she served up her savory meals. If he approached her, she turned and walked the other way. If he smiled at her, she frowned in return. Her rebuff hurt him the worst of all.

The week wore on, the nights in the men's quarters routinely ending now with Onesimus adding a little more to each chapter of his adventures, and soon it was time for the weekly gathering of believers. At first, Onesimus knew that some of the believers who had gathered were uneasy in his presence and didn't know how to react to his return.

Onesimus had sat on the right side of the window on the porch before he left because Apollonia sat on the left side. He sat there now because he was involved in this life of belief and wanted to be as close to the center of things as he could get. He was saddened, though, to see Apollonia move away as soon as he sat down.

Even so, it was during this meeting that things began to change for the better.

A young woman stood and began to sing a song praising God's forgiveness. "Our Father of the morning we praise your holy Name!" she sang. "For when we wander far away, you love us just the same! You welcome home the wanderer and open wide the door, Your grace and mercy never rest, they ride upon your wings of forgiveness!", a prophecy about restoring fellowship to one who had stumbled and another song about welcoming home the wayward sinner. It was then that Philemon stood and took a parchment roll from his girdle.

"A while ago, a young unbelieving slave of mine, stole a purse of gold and ran away. I had begun to care for this slave and it was a very painful thing to realize that he seemingly had no regard for me. This week, Onesimus returned to my home bearing this letter from our dear friend, Paulus.

"Since he has been back, many of his fellow-slaves have forgiven him and accepted him back. But I have seen that some of them still bear grudges against him. They shun him, refuse to speak to him and walk away when he approaches them. This is wrong. If these slaves who do this are unbelievers I understand that forgiveness might come hard to them. But for those of you who name the name of Christ, forgiveness should be a natural part of who you are. After all, God forgave you and continues to forgive you time after time when you stumble. Yeshua warned that if you could not forgive others, then He could not forgive you. Let me read what Paulus has written to me concerning our returned brother."

As he began to read the missive, Philemon glanced up at Onesimus and smiled. Then he returned his eyes to Paulus' epistle and read.

"*This letter is from Paulus, in prison for preaching the Good News about Christ Jesus, and from our brother Timothy. It is written to Philemon, our much-loved co-worker, and to our sister Apphia and to Archippus, a fellow soldier of the cross. I am also writing to the church that meets in your house . . .*"

As Philemon concluded the letter complete with Paulus' promise that he was soon to visit Colossae, Onesimus felt a soft movement near his back. He turned to look over his shoulder and saw Apollonia smiling tentatively at him. He stretched his left arm behind him and beckoned her to come join him at the window. She didn't speak a word but the tears in her eyes said it all and Onesimus smiled.

When the meeting was concluded, Philemon smiled to see several of the slaves who had been avoiding Onesimus were gathered around talking to him. Some, especially those who were not believers, were having more difficulty with it but many had taken the messages of the gathering to heart and were beginning to accept this particular prodigal's return.

"HO! Onesimus!" Philemon's good-natured greeting brought a quick smile to Onesimus' face. "Are you ready for the harvest?"

Onesimus raised his eyebrows comically and made a little face.

Philemon shoved a plateful of food into Onesimus' hands. "Well, boy! You'd better get ready. From what I see in the groves it's going to be a bumper crop!"

αω

CHAPTER THREE

As harvest drew near, Onesimus once again found himself knee-deep in scrolls, reeds, iron oxide, and lamp soot. His job started with creating the ink, both red and black, that he would need to record his master's transactions and the harvest totals. As he labored over this mundane task it began to dawn on him that he would soon no longer be knee deep in tools but rather he would be neck-deep in olives and then would come the winter.

Since he had left Philemon's household before winter had set in, he still had no idea what his winter assignment might be. Whatever it was, he was pretty certain it would be a great slow-down from harvest-time and he looked forward to it and to the chance to get to know the fascinating Apollonia better . . . much better. The very thought of getting to know Apollonia brought a smile to his face. As he sat on his stool mixing his inks and preparing his writing implements, his thoughts carried him away until his hands stilled and his eyes drifted shut as he imagined how his next meeting with Apollonia would go.

Philemon looked over and saw Onesimus with the silly grin on his face, his head tilted to one side and his eyes closed and shook his head. He knew exactly what his Useful One was thinking about. Before Onesimus' unhappy departure, Philemon had seen the quiet smiles and small touches exchanged. He had witnessed the two of them "walking out" together in the cool of the evening. Nevertheless, he also knew there was work that needed to be done and he did the only thing he could think of to bring Onesimus back to the task without letting on that he knew Onesimus was daydreaming. He stood up from his stool and, with a sharp push of his arm, sent the stool clattering to the bedrock and packed-dirt floor.

Onesimus jumped, as Philemon knew he would, and returned to the business at hand. Philemon, with a secret little grin, picked up his stool and set it upright. Then, he strolled out the door and moved off toward the groves where the olives hung heavy, begging for harvest. He had every confidence that Onesimus would continue to work without his immediate supervision and he needed to stop in on his mother-in-law. She had had a cold and he wanted to keep an eye out to ensure it didn't turn into something more dangerous.

Philemon had been right in his assessment of Onesimus' willingness to work without supervision and it was nearly an hour later when Quintin came tearing through the door as he had in days of old.

"Onesimus!" he shouted agitatedly. "Father wants you right away There is something wrong with Grandmother. She's been ill for a while and Father said to tell you to come quickly!"

The slave set aside his reed and capped the inks so they wouldn't dry out and was out the door in a few seconds. Young and sound of limb, Onesimus and Quintin set out at a sprint, crossing the field that lay between the main house and the cottage Quintin's grandmother occupied.

Entering the small room, Onesimus was greeted by Philemon who whispered urgently, "Come this way. Mother Rhais is very ill and needs our prayers." He glanced over at Quintin. "Don't tell Mother about this. She will fret and fuss and worry herself sick. If her mother gets worse, we will inform her but for now, we will pray and ask the Lord to raise her up."

Quintin nodded his understanding and the three of them moved to the bedside and began to pray. Mother Rhais was a believer but was currently in no shape to do more than to agree with the prayers of the others gathered around her couch. Her fever had spiked in the night and she had spent the early morning hours sitting on the side of her bed struggling to breathe. Her face was tinged with gray and her lips were, too.

Philemon, as head of the house and Master, led the first prayer with Quintin following and Onesimus finishing. As they completed their prayer, they noticed that the patient was a little easier in her breathing and her color was returning but she was still not well.

Philemon dipped a cloth in cool water and began bathing his mother-in-law's forehead as he started to speak. "Mother Rhais, I think we should call in a physician. He would be able to leach you and remove the bad humors that are troubling you."

Rhais shook her head adamantly. "No leaches, no physicians! They know less about a woman's body than I do! This has nothing to do with bad humors. It is nothing that some hot willow bark tea won't cure. That and prayer is all I need. Send my daughter to me and she will prepare what is needed."

Philemon looked at Onesimus as if asking him what he thought. Onesimus, forever more the "good" slave, widened his eyes, tipped his head to the side and gave a little shrug; refusing to make a decision for his Master that only the Master should make.

Lips and eyes narrowing to slits, Philemon shook his head slightly and said, "As you wish, Mother Rhais. I shall send Apphia right away. May God be with you."

The trio took their leave and hurried back to their duties.

"Quintin, go tell your mother that her mother would like her to come brew some willow bark tea for her, but have her stop in here before she goes," Philemon told his son. The worried frown, though not as deep as it had been was still present as he sat on a small bench beside the entrance to the olive press.

It was less than five minutes when Apphia approached the olive press and crossed to Philemon's seat.

Philemon rose and took her hands in his. Gazing into her eyes, he spoke gently, "Dearest, your mother has had some difficulty breathing. Quintin, I and Onesimus went and prayed with her and she improved but she is not well and refuses the services of a physician. She insists that willow bark tea and you will be all she needs to recover but I'm afraid it isn't that simple this time. Try to persuade her to see a physician. Otherwise it may be the end of her."

Apphia took in a deep breath, "Husband, I know you think I can persuade my mother to do anything but I'm certain making her see a physician is beyond even my abilities. I will try but it would be a miracle like unto the raising of Lazarus! She fears physicians so . . . and considering what they did to Father, it's no wonder!"

She left the press and crossed the field to her mother's cottage and Philemon was left to remember what his wife had told him of his father-in-law's last days.

Vindur had been a hale and hearty forty-year-old with a teen-aged daughter and a happy marriage when he had been found beside the road with no sign of what was wrong except he was insensible to everything around him. His friends brought him to his couch and Rhais had sent Apphia to summon the town's physician.

After a short examination, the physician announced the man had a severe brain fever brought about by an overabundance of blood within his brain. He immediately applied ten or more leaches to Vindur's scalp as Rhais and Apphia watched their husband and father grow paler and weaker. After the first few hours, Rhais began to object to the leaches and told the physician she wanted him to take his treatments and leave, but he was adamant that he would continue to treat his patient because she was merely a woman and had no say in the matter. It was shortly after this argument that the physician decided to augment his leaches by bleeding Vindur. He took hold of Vindur's arm and sliced across his wrist. It was a matter of minutes and Rhais was a widow and Apphia was fatherless.

Philemon closed his eyes and shook his head. Perhaps Rhais was right to be doubtful of the physician's art.

About the time Philemon stepped through the door to go back to work, Blandina came tearing across the yard as if the devil himself were chasing her. "Father! Father! We have a visitor and you *must* come immediately!"

Philemon was shocked that his little girl would speak so to him. "Now see here, girl! You can't tell me what I must and mustn't do! I . . ."

"Don't be too hard on the girl! She was simply conveying my request in a slightly more forceful way!" the visitor laughed as he stepped into the press.

Hearing the familiar voice, Onesimus jumped from his stool and, forgetting his place completely, grabbed Philemon's arm, shouting, "Paulus! It's Paulus!" He grabbed the Apostle in a bear hug and danced merrily around the room with him.

Paulus was laughing and hugging as well until, winded, he slowed down and stopped, asking, "And just who might you be, young man?"

Philemon, wisely, had stood back and allowed this demonstration of unalloyed joy continue until it ran its course. Now he stepped forward and gave the man of God a Roman salute.

"I am so glad you have come at last! My gratitude for returning my 'new' slave to me knows no bounds. And now, just as you have arrived . . ."

Apphia entered the room at a run and, panting with effort, grabbed Philemon's arm. "Husband, oh my Husband!" she cried. "Mother has collapsed to the floor and lies there as if she were dead! What shall we do? What *can* we do?"

Paulus looked at Onesimus and said, "Show me the way."

Casting a glance at his master for Philemon's nod, Onesimus led Paulus back to the hut and up to the elderly woman who lay supine on the floor next to a spilled wooden bowl of tea.

Paulus told Onesimus to carry her to her bed where he sat down beside her and began to pray with the power and might of one born out of season but born well. The authority he wielded was awesome to behold and Philemon and Apphia who had both followed in his wake just stood watching as the power of God was made manifest in that small cabin. It was so clearly present that all in attendance could have sworn the building itself shook.

Rhais lay still and unknowing until the powerful words of the follower of Christ were spoken, "Thou foul spirit of disease, in the name of Christ Jesus I command thee to remove thy hands from this woman of God. Sickness and death, by the authority of Jesus the Christ I command thee to flee and to have no more power in this family!"

Immediately, Rhais breathed in sharply and opened her eyes. Color flooded her face and lips and she smiled. "You see, Philemon? I told you a little willow bark tea was all I needed!"

Laughter and joy entered that small home at that moment and, from then on, would have a permanent place by the hearth.

αω

CHAPTER FOUR

Onesimus awoke just before the Lord's Day rising call was given. He wasn't sure whether it was because he was getting attuned to his work/sleep schedule or if he was just excited because his beloved Paulus was going to bring greetings to the Body today.

Either way, he was awake and giving morning praise to God when Justin walked through the quarters ringing a bell and shouting, "Rise up! Rise up! Give glory to the God of the Universe and praise to His Son. The day has dawned and we may yet serve Him another day!"

The familiar call and bell took Onesimus back to the first Lord's Day when, upon rising, he had seen no sign of anything to break his fast with. He smiled wryly as he remembered wondering if he was going to be left without food all day! How wonderful to know better and to be back in the comfort of familiar things. With these thoughts foremost in his mind, he arose and bathed and slipped into a particular robe he saved for sacred occasions.

When all was ready, he and the other slaves stepped out the door and headed for the front of the main house where they could see people almost streaming down the road. Each family group carried a large wicker basket filled with something for the table. As they arrived, the believers placed their baskets on the table from the cook house and began visiting and greeting each other as brothers and sisters commonly do, with hugs and cheek-kisses.

At the appointed time, Philemon stepped forward. "My dear brothers and sisters, welcome. I am pleased to tell you that our long-awaited visit from Paulus has finally arrived."

He paused as a general murmur of joy rose from the listeners.

"Paulus arrived two days ago, just in time to pray for my mother-in-law," here, he nodded toward the woman standing beside him, "who was lying as one dead until Paulus came along. It is with gratitude we praise the almighty Father for sparing her life and sending us this beloved father of the church to teach us this day.

"Now, I invite you all to enjoy this fine meal and the Lord's Supper which will be included before the worship starts. Let us ask the Father's blessing …

"Christ Jesus, Creator of the universe, we come to You in thankfulness for Your bounty and Your blessings. Thank You for bringing our dear teacher to us safely and bless these victuals to the good of our bodies and our spirits. Amen."

Everyone gathered round the tables and began to select from the roast kid, cheeses, barley and wheat breads, olives, figs, and grapes that had loaded the table until it almost groaned under the weight.

Soon the fast had been thoroughly broken and the believers began to gather round the table to remember the sacrifice of the Lord.

Philemon asked that Paulus speak, and he began, "It is important that we remember the death and resurrection of our Lord Christ and it is our privilege to do so today."

As Paulus spoke, Philemon took a bottle of wine and poured some into a precious silver chalice and then he took a loaf of barley bread and tore it into bite-sized pieces.

"Each of us must indeed ask the Holy Spirit to search our hearts and reveal to us any sins we must be cleansed of before partaking of this very special remembrance. Let each of us now do so; for to drink of this cup and eat of this bread without a clean heart brings us to sickness and some even to death. Let us prepare our hearts."

Silence reigned as those who believed sought out forgiveness for any slight stain on their souls and others stood by, albeit uncomfortably for some, and watched this ritual.

When the saints moved toward the table, Paulus lifted the chalice and handed it to the first man. He sipped and passed the chalice to the woman behind him and took a piece of the proffered bread. Slave and free partook together without equivocation.

"On that night," Paulus intoned, "Christ took the cup and gave to His disciples saying, 'Take, drink ye, for this is my blood which is poured out for the remission of your sins.' In the same way, He broke the bread and passed it saying, 'This is my body, broken for you. As often as you do this, remember me.'"

As each completed the ritual, they gave Paulus and Philemon a hug and moved off toward the house where the meeting was soon to start. Onesimus wasn't sure, but he felt as if his hug from Paulus was just a little longer than most and that made his heart glad.

Apollonia was in her usual place and Philemon smiled and nudged Paulus as he nodded at Onesimus who was almost running across the yard to sit beside her.

Paulus asked the question without a word, simply by raising his eyebrows.

"Oh, my, yes!" Philemon answered. "Apollonia is a perfect match for our dear, impetuous brother! She is steady and full of grace."

Paulus just nodded approvingly and moved toward the house where he would speak. By the time he arrived, a song had already started.

The melody, sung by a dark-voiced man this day, drifted out across the lawn and other believers accompanied the words with wordless harmonies that still brought a thrill to Onesimus' spine every time he heard it.

"Jesus, I bring an offering to You. An offering of praise for Your sovereign might.

"When I remember the eternal life You have purchased for those who follow You," the song went, "My soul thrills with joy untold."

"Honor and Glory reside upon Your face and we bow before Your Heavenly Majesty in adoration."

"Holy, Holy, Holy; You are worthy of our praise."

After several more minutes, the song died out and spontaneous prayer rose to the Heavens followed by a prophecy and then another song, this one started by a middle-aged woman, "O Father of all believers, we bow before you in worship!

"Your Holy Son You gave to purchase a sinful mankind,

"Before we knew You, You knew and loved us.

"Blind we were and fearful of all around us,

"But You lifted the veil of darkness and banished fear from our hearts.

"Exalt the Lord all You Heavens and Praise Him all those who walk after Him."

Onesimus raised his voice with the others and sent praises soaring skyward as his spirit lifted him beyond this earthly plane and his tongue began to speak words he did not know. He sang and spoke for several minutes, saying whatever the Spirit told him to say.

What unbelieving observers sometimes didn't understand was that he could have stopped anytime ... he wasn't "possessed" or "out of control" . . . but why would a believer who had yielded his all to the Holy Spirit ever refuse to say what the Spirit whispered into his soul? When he was finished an elderly woman arose speaking words of comfort and peace to the troubled.

When the Holy Spirit had comforted and touched those who were in need, Paulus rose to his feet to speak.

"Today I bring news of Rome to you. Believers there have been coming under harsher and more difficult persecution daily. About a fortnight after our brother Onesimus left the city the fire you have heard of broke out, wiping out half the city. At first, all would blame Nero for the conflagration but that old fox found a way to shift the accusations to the Christians of the city. It was this that brought the first serious attack against a group of believers led by my brother Apostle, Petros. I was told this story by a young girl who had visited the group shortly before.

"She said word had come that the authorities were searching for leaders of the church to punish the Christians for the fire and put an end to the church's growth. When Petros was taken, they brought him to the place where he was to be crucified and he begged to be allowed to be martyred upside down because he felt unworthy to die as his Lord had.

"At the time I heard this story, I had been drawn away to other regions by the Holy Spirit and it was during these travels that my path crossed with the girl who lived in Puteoli. She had heard the story from her governess who had followed her back to her home."

Onesimus began feeling the familiar buzzing in his head that, for him, signaled a chance to recognize God at work.

Paulus continued, "Martina then told me that she had been a believer for some time, but her parents had just come to The Way after a member of their caravan prayed for a fellow-traveler and saved his life. She feared that these new believers would be unable to withstand the trials that might come and asked that I ask every believer I met to pray not only for her parents but for all the Christians of Rome that they can endure the coming days and I promised I would.

"This is a firmly rooted body of believers and for that reason, I believe we need to enter into powerful prayer for those who serve our Lord in persecution."

Without another word, every believer in the group began to pray. Some prayed in their native tongue and some in a foreign tongue and some . . . many, in fact . . . prayed in the tongues of angels.

Intercession was deep and long and all who believed participated but even deep intercession must cease after a while and, as the prayers died down, Paulus spoke.

"And now I bring you this teaching for life from our Lord.

"The news of persecutions may very well bring hesitation and doubt to the strongest among us and yet, there is no reason to fear. Just as Christ Jesus conquered death for Himself and for us, so we will find there is just a step beyond the threshold of death to enter into the presence of God the Father and we shall behold the face of the One Who died for us. We shall bow before Him and cast our crowns at His feet, for He alone is worthy to be the Ruler of Heaven and Earth.

"Before that great day we need to rest in Him. We need to trust in His promises and His provision for us. God's people rebelled against Him long ago while in the wilderness and God made his people to wander in the desert for forty years. And later, He spoke to those who disobeyed Him and told them they would never enter His rest. But it was because of their unbelief they could not enter in.

"God's promise that believers may enter His rest still stands, so we ought to tremble with fear that some of you may fail to experience that rest. Just as the Israelites could enter no rest because of their unbelief, it would be *your* unbelief that would bar you from entering into the rest afforded the followers of our Lord.

"This good news, that God has prepared this rest, has been announced to us as well as to those long-ago people who couldn't enter because of unbelief. This rest was prepared by Him when He rested on the seventh day.

"Since His people failed to trust Him, they could no longer enter His rest and God set another time for us to enter His rest. That time is today, as David wrote: 'Today when you hear His voice, do not harden your hearts.'

"Now if Joshua had succeeded in giving them this rest, God would not have spoken about another day of rest still to come. So, there is a special rest still waiting for the people of God, for all who have entered into that rest have rested from their labors.

"What God has provided for us is a rest that comes from entering into Christ Jesus, Himself. He is our rest. We can rest, certain that all the events in our lives are the work of Jesus and have been planned from the beginning of time. We need not struggle to labor for our faith. Our faith will spontaneously lead us to work for that harvest of souls Christ spoke of when He said, 'The fields are white unto harvest'. We need not strive for our rest. If that were the case, we would be working, not resting. He will provide all we need to enter into that dearest of rests and we can then labor for him with peace in our hearts.

"It is true that we must strive for holiness so that we can stand before the King of Kings and know that we have done all we can. But the first step in striving for holiness is to rest in His grace and know that He Who has begun a good work in us will be faithful to complete it. Although we may stumble and fail Him sometimes, still we can remain in His rest by understanding that our failings, although grievous, can be repented in the twinkling of an eye and our holiness be restored to us just as quickly.

"Now, and from now on, remember that our gift from God the Father is rest. And when we learn to trust Him for the rest, the fleshly striving by which we have struggled to win His rest will fade away and we will know the peace that passes all understanding."

When Paulus sat down, another song erupted and after that, Philemon announced that the meeting was over and everyone dispersed toward the table in the yard.

As Onesimus walked over to the table, he felt a tap on his shoulder. He turned around and, standing before him, was a short, muscular man with ebony skin. He spoke in a foreign language and Onesimus shook his head, indicating that he did not understand. The man tilted his head to one side and spoke in Greek and Onesimus found that he had to listen closely to understand the man through his thick accent.

"How came thee to speak to me in my native tongue and yet you claim to not know the language of Egypt?"

Onesimus again shook his head, "I do not speak Egyptian. When did you hear me and what did I say?"

"You told the story of this god-man, Christos, Who died for my sins and Who conquered death by coming to life again so that I might have life. It was during the meeting. I am Revocatus, a new slave in the home of Jovita and do not understand much but I would like to hear more of this Christos," the man replied.

"Today, for the believers here, there is no division between slave and free, so come gather some food and we will sit together and I will tell you of marvelous works too wondrous to deny," Onesimus replied as he heaped the new slave's trencher full and led him to the place on the porch where he had first heard the stories of Jesus.

CHAPTER FIVE

P hilemon was very tired. As he had predicted, the harvest had almost doubled from the year before and even he had taken his own turn at beating the trees to knock down the olives. His shoulders and arms ached from the unaccustomed swinging of the long pole and the jarring impact with the branches. While he was a strong man, these were muscles he seldom used in his everyday life and his forearms and upper chest muscles were making their displeasure known to him.

Onesimus had been too busy counting and tracking to spend time under the trees. He had offered to let Philemon do the bookkeeping while he went into the groves to do harvest work itself, but Philemon refused. His clerk was good at what he did and Philemon enjoyed the occasional day of physical labor.

Finally, the last day of harvest passed and tomorrow was the big end-of-harvest celebration. All the surrounding community, all the believers from the Lord's Day meetings, all the slaves and the residents living near Colossae that Philemon and Apphia knew had been invited to join in the celebration. Philemon expected that the yard and adjoining fields would be filled with friends and neighbors and maybe even a few strangers brought in by curiosity.

He knew that the workers in the cook house had already been preparing a feast like none ever seen in the region before. There were all the standard items of bread, roasted eggs, wheels of cow's cheese and blocks of goat cheese, and baskets full of grapes and figs. Beyond that, Philemon had managed to import rare delicacies from other regions. A grain called couscous from northern Africa over which one would spread stew, and from Egypt a dish called falafel made of chickpeas and cooked in oil. To top off the meal there would be baklava and sweetened and spiced breads. It was going to be so huge that the evening meal tonight would be taken from the pots and baskets and ewers that held the banquet and wouldn't even be missed. Beyond that, the cooks would continue their efforts throughout tomorrow morning, roasting lambs, a pig, and goats over spits in the yard and cooking chickens and ducks in the large ovens inside the cookhouse. When all the meats were cooking, then and only then would they have a few hours to rest before the meats were ready and the merriment began in the late afternoon.

Some of the field hands and men who worked at building and maintaining the grounds were pounding pegs into new table tops and then placing the table tops upside down on the ground. Next, they carved out a corresponding hole in the top of the legs and then flipped the legs upside down, starting the pegs into the holes which were barely large enough. The men with the mallets would then pound on the bottoms of the legs, forcing the legs down onto the pegs. After that came the addition of a couple of braces on each end of the table. The table was then flipped onto its legs and tested for stability. When it met the approval of the man supervising, it was placed in the yard to hold the coming provender. Only once all day did Philemon see a table fail the exacting test the supervisor had devised. Each table was pushed and pulled from the ends. Then they were pushed and pulled from the sides. Lastly, they endured the weight of two of the four men working on them as they climbed up on top of them and literally jumped up and down.

The table that failed survived every test except the last one, collapsing underneath the two men who jumped clear of the chaos when they heard the *CRACK!* of braces failing. They began laughing and slapping each other on the back as they collected themselves and removed the ruined table.

Philemon was taking a well-earned break, relaxing on the porch and watching the men work, when he saw something that caused his eyebrows to raise and a large grin to cross his face.

Out beyond the olive press, in the edge of the olive grove, Onesimus was walking and he wasn't alone. Beside him, with her usual grace and dignity, Apollonia looked raptly up into his face as he held forth on some subject she obviously thought was of vital importance. Philemon couldn't hear, of course, what was being said but he could see that it probably wouldn't be long before the former runaway would be coming to him with a very *serious* question.

Of course, Onesimus had no idea what had transpired between Paulus and his master when the Apostle had come to visit and spy out the locale. Plans were afoot that would have sped Onesimus to the decision he himself had so little knowledge he was contemplating! But that was the whole idea behind the secrecy. The olives must be allowed to ripen before they were harvested, or the fruit would produce a very poor-quality oil . . . so, too, must romance be allowed to ripen before the fruit is harvested.

After the grand party tomorrow evening, it would be back to work as usual and all of Philemon's male slaves, including Onesimus, would be occupied at physical labor for the next month or more. Even Philemon would be helping as the wagons underwent their yearly repairs and the house and outbuildings were whitewashed and the grounds were prepared for the winter.

While it was true that Greek winters were moderate in temperature, it was also true that storms were almost daily occurrences along with strong winds and fog. This meant that if Philemon wanted to keep his home and outbuildings durable, new coats of whitewash and repairs to shutters and doors had to be completed before the infamous "Season of Storms" was upon them.

Above all else, all the animals had to be cared for and their shelters had to be repaired and stocked with feed for the winter months. The cows, horses, sheep, and goats all shared a stable together. The pigs were separated because of their love of mud, and chickens, ducks and other fowl were housed in a coop not far from the cook house.

After all this was finished, Philemon would select a few pigs and a cow to be slaughtered and smoked and then all would be ready for the winter and life would slow down to its winter pace.

But before all this activity began, there was the harvest gathering. *A festival,* Philemon thought with satisfaction (as he did every year at this time), *the likes of which has never before been seen around here!*

αω

CHAPTER SIX

T he party was going well. A couple of the female slaves had taken the children into the side yard where they were playing games. Their joy at just being alive demonstrated how ecstatic a child can be for no apparent reason.

Apphia, as the Mistress of the home, stood near the cook house, supervising the movement of food dishes from the kitchen to the table and watching the children. Her heart was lifted to see how much fun they were having. A slight frown slipped across her face as she realized she could see her daughter Blandina but Quintin wasn't visible. She knew, in her head, that Blandina's twin, Quintin was older than most of the children at play and yet, in her heart, he was still the little boy with blue-black curls and the scent of the summer sun on his skin that she had loved and cared for since she had given him life.

She was almost ready to call Philemon over and ask him about their seemingly absent son when she finally caught sight of him. He wasn't with the children, but he had a companion beside him. They were walking along the edge of the olive grove and Apphia couldn't make out who it was from this distance, but she *was* able to see she was a female . . . and the way she leaned in to Quintin . . . the way she reached over and touched his arm . . . suddenly the knowledge flooded through Apphia that the little boy with the winsome grin and beautiful eyelashes was gone and gone forever.

Her hand fluttered up to her breast and she gasped slightly when she saw Quintin and the girl come together in a tender but innocent kiss. She looked away, feeling as if she had been spying on the couple and yet she was *still* willing to give one eye and several teeth to know who had captured her son's heart!

"So!" Apphia jumped at the loudly spoken word. "You've finally seen our boy with his new project!" Philemon said as he stepped up beside her.

"You've known?" she asked in astonishment. Quintin always had come to *her* with his secrets and new interests. *She* had been his closest confidant. Now, as teenaged boys were wont to do, it was obvious he was turning to his father.

"Oh! I've known for some time, dearest. He made me promise not to tell you because he wanted to wait until he was sure. He knows he isn't ready to marry her but he's looking forward. I'd guess he's going to her father soon to begin the betrothal."

"Husband! Who is it?" she asked. "I wasn't able to see!"

Philemon smiled and took her hands in his. "I guess since you've seen what you've seen the promise to not tell you is null, now so . . . it's Quinta. Remember how they used to laugh about being twins because of the similarity of their names? How they played together after the Lord's Day meetings? He tells me he's loved her since they were both small children."

He reached out and wiped a tear from his beloved wife's cheek. "Now, sweet one, don't go on so! After all, he *is* fourteen! It's time he started looking at girls. And it will be a couple of years before the betrothal takes place."

Her words came on the breath of a sigh, "I know. It's the way of things, but he still seems so young to me!"

Philemon wrapped his arms around her waist and nuzzled her neck for a moment. "'Twill be fine, Apphia. I promise, 'twill be fine."

Λ Ω

Young love was definitely in the air that night. The proof would stand with knees knocking and voice shaking before Philemon the next day and ask permission to wed.

"Sir, as you know, Apollonia and I have been walking together ever since my return," Onesimus started. "I find her to be intelligent, beautiful, charming, a good conversationalist, beautif—".

"I know Apollonia, probably better than you do. After all she's MY slave!" Philemon interrupted gruffly.

Onesimus gave a little start, unnerved by the abrupt response. Was Philemon going to refuse him permission? Worse yet, would he threaten to sell one of them if this romance didn't end? Moments passed as he considered saying no more and leaving. His mind rushed back to his first day here, when Justin advised him that Philemon would allow good marriages among his slaves. Had that changed? Would his running away make Philemon consider him not a good candidate for Apollonia's husband? His tongue felt like it had swollen to twice its normal size and his throat was as dry as a bed of ash. He stood still and could say nothing.

"If you have something to say, Onesimus, you'd better say it quickly!" Philemon spoke gruffly. "I'm a busy man!" He turned his face away from Onesimus before the slave could see the grin that was spreading across his face.

Onesimus stood remembering the fear he had felt when Philemon had first bought him from the slaver. He recalled with what shame and trepidation he had approached Philemon's house when he returned from his run. He wished he was back in either of those places rather than to be here. Nevertheless, *this* difficult task could win him a prize more precious than rubies. He stood his ground and struggled to clear his throat.

"Sir!" the word came out almost as a shout and he started over. "Sir, I love Apollonia and I would like to marry her. I don't know why, but she loves me, too! She is a fit for me. She is strong where I am weak and she has the courage to admit her weaknesses and allow my strength to help her in those areas, Master," Onesimus stopped and looked down at the floor. Philemon wasn't even looking at him . . . he wasn't paying attention! How could he get through to this man how much he *needed* to wed the lovely Apollonia?

"Onesimus!" Philemon turned to show his smile to the slave. "You have made this much more difficult for yourself than it had to be! All you had to do was utter that single phrase, 'I would like to marry her.' I've known you were made for each other the first time I saw you two mooning around the olive presses!

"Harvest is over and the winter preparations will take about six to eight weeks to complete. We will announce your betrothal next Lord's

Day and you may select your bridal date for sometime after the autumn work is completed."

Onesimus almost fell to his knees with relief. He almost danced across the floor with joy. He grabbed Philemon in a most unseemly bear hug and swung him around in a circle all the while shouting, "Thank you, Master! Thank you, Sir!"

"STOP!" Philemon roared in good humor. "All this affection should be going toward your betrothed, should it not? Go! I think she can be spared from the cook house for a goodly span seeing as how we are still eating from last night's festivities!"

Philemon had never seen a man turn and run as fast as Onesimus did as he clambered up the steps to the cookhouse door shouting, "Apollonia! Apollonia! Come with me. Master has given me permission to talk with you!"

He grabbed her hand and pulled her out of the cookhouse so quickly she hadn't had time to cover her beautiful auburn hair. "Onesimus! What are you doing?" she exclaimed. "I need to help with the midday prepar—"

"No you don't!" the Useful One interrupted. "The Master has given us time to discuss a few things that truly need to be discussed right away." As he was speaking he was tugging Apollonia along with him, pulling her further from the cookhouse and closer to the olive grove where he felt they might find a measure of privacy. He didn't stop until they were within the bounds of the orchard and well away from the prying eyes his abrupt kidnapping of the head cook had attracted.

Without saying a word, he slipped one arm around her waist. With his other hand, he brushed the auburn waves away from her face. Auburn waves he had never had the privilege to see before, let alone touch. Her hair was soft and shining and he imagined it spread out on a couch next to him.

He quickly removed his hand as if it were burned. He knew he needed to back up and halt the progress of his thoughts before they could sully this tenderness he felt with emotions best left for the wedding night.

"I talked to the Master, my darling dear," he began. "He gave me his blessing to come to you and ask you. I love you with everything I am. I know I have nothing to offer you but my faithful devotion and steadfast heart but if you would have me as your husband . . . if you would consent to be my wife . . . I would never, *ever* cause you to weep. I would never, *ever* give to you a sense of abandonment or loneliness and I promise to always, *always* remain your own true love."

His heart thundering in his chest, Onesimus stood looking into his beloved's striking gray eyes.

She stood looking up at him, her eyes wide and her mouth open.

She stood that way for so long that Onesimus began to wonder, *Oh no! I misunderstood! She doesn't love me! She doesn't want me! She's going to say no! What will I do? How can I remain here if she turns me down?*

He was almost bowled over when she abruptly stepped forward and wrapped her arms around him. "Yes!" She said with joy. "Oh! Yes!"

A few moments of heaven, Onesimus thought as he held her close. *And then we must return to the everyday.*

"Master says we can announce our betrothal at the next Lord's Day meeting," he said softly into the magnificent chestnut waves. "We need to talk with him about where we will live. I believe the three family cabins are already occupied . . . and we need to . . ."

"We *need,*" Apollonia interrupted, "to enjoy this moment without fretting about the next step. I'm sure the Master will talk with us before the Lord's Day."

And so they stood. Arms around each other, Onesimus' face buried in the lovely, soft waves of her hair and Apollonia's face buried in Onesimus' chest.

αω

CHAPTER SEVEN

*H*e was in a ship with his father and brother. They were having a fine time together, but a storm was coming. The sky darkened and the waves rose high, towering over their vessel. It wasn't long before the boat was tossing as if it were a small stick on the Tiber. The sailors were cursing and calling on the gods for help. There was a loud screech and CRACK! and the stern of the ship was torn away and sunk quickly with half the crew. He knew there was no hope. There were only a few seconds in which to grab something that would float before the bow of the ship followed the stern to its watery grave. He grabbed the nearest thing—a splintered plank that had been ripped from the hull and flung through the air onto the deck.

Suddenly he tasted salt water and his brother and father were clinging to the plank with him. But the weight of three grown men was too much for the little plank. Soon Protos and his father were crying that they would all drown if something weren't done quickly. He heard his father shouting to Protos, "Push him off! Better that you and I should live and Onesimus perish than that we all die!"

Onesimus released his grip on the board and shouted to his father, "He doesn't need to push me off. My God will protect me. I love you both and will pray you make it safely to shore, for you have yet to hear!"

A giant wave rose up and crashed over his head and he gasped . . .
and awoke.

Just then, another giant wave struck him in the face and he laughed quietly as he realized the rains had come and the roof was leaking just above his bed.

Onesimus sat up and thought about his dream. He remembered it from before, when he first arrived at Philemon's house. Why would it come back to him now? But no, it wasn't exactly the same. In this version, he wasn't fighting for a place on the floating board. Instead he willingly gave up his place so his father and brother could live. What did he say to them? "You have yet to hear!"

An ache arose in his heart. He realized that since his conversion all his thoughts toward his family had been loving, but until now he had never thought to go to them and ask their forgiveness for the uncharitable thoughts he had had toward them. There had never been a question about *forgiving* them. It had never crossed his mind to withhold forgiveness! It had hardly crossed his mind that he *needed* to forgive them. After all, if his father hadn't sold him, he never would have heard of The Way, nor met the woman who would be his wife, would not have run from his Master, never would have met Paulus, he might never have come to accept the Anointed One, Yeshua! He would be forever in his father's debt for what he had done.

But now, Onesimus began to realize that he needed to tell his father what he had learned and how he felt. His father must be living under a terrible burden of pain and sorrow and it was Onesimus' duty to release him by returning to the family home and telling him about the events of the last few years.

He lay back down and cradled his head on his folded arm.

He really wanted to go to his father, but he was a slave. He was subject to his Master's needs. And now he was planning a wedding besides! How could he find a chance . . . before he could finish the thought, he returned to his slumbers and slept through until the morning.

Λ Ω

Philemon, Onesimus and Apollonia sat together on the porch. Six weeks before, the betrothal announcement had been greeted with great good cheer just before the believers settled down for the Lord's Day meeting.

Since then the blessed couple had worked with a will to help prepare the Master's property for the coming winter blast. Now the work was over. The buildings had been repaired (including the slave quarters' leaking roof over Onesimus' couch!) and painted and the animals had been properly sheltered. Those animals destined to be the household provender for the stormy times ahead had been slaughtered and smoked or salted and now hung in the smokehouse or rested in their salt barrels waiting to be consumed.

Now it was time for promises to be kept and plans to be made.

"My only question, Onesimus, concerning your nuptials is this: Do you want to take the trip after you marry or do you wish to wait until your return to wed?" Philemon said.

Onesimus peered at him as if he had never seen him before. What did he mean "take the trip"? What trip? He had opened his mouth to ask when Philemon continued, "You have done an excellent job of straightening your paths from the moment you went away until your conversion. But you and I both know you have yet to talk with your family and I believe God has been talking to you about this for some time, now." He raised his eyebrows in inquiry.

"Well, yes sir. I've been having dreams about my family lately and I know I need to go see them. But I also know that I am subject to your will and so I've said nothing through the winter preparations," Onesimus admitted.

"Nothing to do with reluctance, is it?" Philemon asked bluntly.

"Oh, no!" came the reply. "I *want* to go to them and tell them of The Way! But with winter coming and," he glanced over at Apollonia, "the wedding. . ." she cast her eyes to the ground and, even with her veil in place Onesimus could tell she was blushing.

"Well," Philemon said quickly. "You've two choices, as I see it. You can marry and then take the trip. Apollonia would be perfectly safe here until your return, or you can put off the wedding until your return . . ."

This time it was Apollonia who interrupted. "Well, Master . . . Onesimus . . . there *is* another choice!" she said quietly. "We could marry and then both of us go!" When she realized what she had said, she looked stricken. "I'm so sorry, Master! I didn't mean it like . . ."

Philemon shook his head and smiled. "I know you well enough to know you could go together and you would return to me without fail. My concern if you accompany him is that the journey could be arduous and . . ." he hesitated and blushed himself as he considered his next words. ". . . for a newly married young lady it might be . . . especially difficult."

"What I had thought was that whichever suggestion you accepted, you could stay here and spend your time preparing your new home."

Onesimus reached out and took Apollonia's hand. They had wondered together what kind of quarters they would have with all the family cots already occupied.

Philemon paused and tilted his head to the left, squinting his eyes with his smile. "My father's cottage is in good repair and Quintin and Quinta won't be ready for it for several years. Do you think that would do you?"

The young couple could barely contain their excitement. A whole cottage to themselves! Their joy flooded their eyes and brought an echo of that joy to Philemon.

Apollonia found her voice first, "Oh! That would be *wonderful!* She exclaimed. "But *could* I go with him?" she asked. "I would like to meet his family."

Philemon smiled and nodded. There was no work during the winter that couldn't just as well be undertaken by other of his slaves. He had several adequate cooks among the women and bookwork in the winter was minimal.

"All right. We shall hold the celebration as part of the Lord's Day Service a fortnight hence. Then you may be on your way the following day and may God be with you on your travels," Philemon said and rose and went into his home, leaving the two young slaves to ponder their great blessing at being brought by God to this home, to this time, and to this kindly Master.

CHAPTER EIGHT

I t was decided that the Lord's Day service would take place and then the marriage of Onesimus and Apollonia would be celebrated. Apollonia would be excused from the service so she could have a little time to prepare. A young girl was deputized to run to the chambers where Apollonia was being dressed to inform them when the service had ended and the wedding could begin.

When Apphia had heard the news, she took Apollonia under her wing and treated her as she would treat her own daughter. She oversaw the ritual bathing and provided a red, dress-like chiton for the bride. She also supplied a fitting veil for the transfer of the bride from Philemon to Onesimus.

(Philemon had been charged with finding a suitable red chiton for Onesimus. This would prove a little more difficult since Philemon, like many young Greeks of the time, had celebrated his wedding thirty years before in the nude.)

Excitement was running high as people enjoyed their fellowship breakfast. The men were saluting Onesimus and laughing with him and, in Apollonia's absence, the women were hugging each other, and everyone was kissing the cheeks of everyone else. Even the children, who had not been informed that this Lord's Day would be different from others, picked up on the joy and they were running and shouting excitedly until their parents called them to order and began to gather for the service.

Just like every groom from time immemorial, Onesimus was jittery, but in in spite of his unraveling nerves he felt an inner calm and peace. The knowledge that, with the exception of his conversion, this would be the very best thing that had ever happened to him calmed him.

He settled in his accustomed place, at the window on the porch, but the absence of his beloved made it hard for him to concentrate.

Thinking back later and trying to remember exactly what had been sung, prophesied, done, and presented during the worship, Onesimus could only shake his head as he remembered exactly nothing—even though the meeting was as uplifting and joyous as always.

At last, it was time. The little girl ran in and announced to the bride that the worship was done and she was summoned. Apollonia stood and Apphia ran a graceful hand over the fine silk veil that covered the bride's anxious face. The slave and the Mistress looked deeply into each other's eyes and turned to walk out of the back of the house. Apphia would walk separately to the front of the house and then go inside.

Onesimus awaited the arrival of his bride on the porch. When she arrived to the sound of applause and a chorus of blessings from the witnesses, he took her hand in his and looked deeply into her soft, grey eyes. Together they walked into the house where they expected Philemon to pronounce a blessing. Their eyes had not yet adjusted to the dim interior when a familiar voice spoke from the area where the messenger usually stood.

"Then Adonai made a woman from the side of the man, and he brought her to the man. The man said, 'This is now bone of my bone and flesh of my flesh; she shall be called woman for she was taken from my flesh.' For this reason a man will leave his father and mother and will be united to his wife and they will become one flesh," Paulus began.

"Love is patient, love is kind, it does not envy, it does not boast, it is not proud. It is not rude, it is not self-seeking, it is not easily angered, and it keeps no record of wrongs. It always protects, always trusts, always hopes, and always perseveres. Love never fails.

"Onesimus, it is time for you to state your desire."

Still blinking in surprise, Onesimus replied, "I desire to take this woman, Apollonia, to be my wife."

Paulus nodded and turned to speak to Philemon who stood beside him. "As the master of this couple, do you consent to this joining and will you hold their bond to be as unbreakable as a freeman's?"

Philemon, taken by surprise by this unexpected question, nodded and responded, "Yes."

Paulus smiled broadly and turned back to the couple.

"In the Hebrew custom I offer you this cup. Crush it beneath your heel, Onesimus."

From nowhere a fragile glass appeared in Paulus's hand. Onesimus took the glass and, placing it upside down on the floor, stomped on it.

"MAZEL TOV!" Paulus shouted. "Oh! That is also a Hebrew custom. It means a little more than "Congratulations" so now, let us all shout . . ."

The crowd had risen to its feet to witness the breaking of the glass and following Paulus's lead shouted, "MAZEL TOV!"

The laughter, music, and general joy commenced and almost everyone began to dance. The feasting and celebration lasted far into the evening and no one noticed when they slipped away.

αω

CHAPTER NINE

"Are you sure you want to come along?" Onesimus was a little worried. When he was contemplating this trip he'd had no qualms about traveling into Colossae and seeing his father . . . but that was before he was a married man! That was before he had a wife to protect and care for . . . and one that was so stubborn!

Apollonia stood with her hands fisted on her hips.

"Oh no, my groom," she smiled. "Two days of marriage is not enough time to make me want a break from you. It isn't that far, Sweetheart. Did you not say your childhood home is only three or four leagues from here? In the city—right? Together we can travel to Colossae, visit with your parents, and return home all in one or two days."

"But there are thieves and murderers along the way, wanting nothing more than to welcome with swords a young, unarmed couple."

"Unarmed?! But I thought the Master loaned you . . ."

"He did, love. But one sword against a band of five or six thieves could not do much damage!"

Apollonia shrugged and smiled, "Then I guess we shall have to rely upon the Sword of the Spirit," and clambering onto the seat of the wagon beside Onesimus, she pulled the top of her outer garment over her head and waved at Quintin, who was trying to build an object of unknown utility in the side yard.

Even though the wagon rattled and bumped over the rougher parts of the road and the dapple gray horse that pulled it seemed more interested in trying to snag an apple from Ignatius' orchard than in holding to his task, the beginning of the journey was pleasant enough. The newlyweds snuggled close on the seat as Onesimus tussled with the horse to keep him on task. After a few minutes of this and, knowing there was a good half-league of orchard to get by, Onesimus halted the wagon and climbed down.

"Husband, what are you doing?"

"Making this trip easier!" he replied with a grin. "Old Ephos, here, has decided he wants an apple, and nothing will do except to get him an apple. I'll inform Ignatius next Lord's day and offer to pay him for the apple."

Apollonia laughed as he climbed the hillock to the nearest tree and plucked a fat apple for the horse. Coming back to the wagon, he approached Ephos with his treat resting on the palm of his outstreched hand from which the horse took it up and, not waiting for his benefactor to regain his seat, trotted off toward Colossae.

By the time they had passed the last apple tree, the couple had fallen into a companionable silence. Barley fields stretched away on their left and a vineyard on the right. The wagon was rumbling along at a good pace and they were waving at the people they saw whether they knew them or not. Their joy in each other could not be contained and it spilled over into an attitude of welcome and camaraderie with everyone they passed.

The sky overhead was a brilliant blue with high, white clouds sailing along. The clouds seemed solid enough that the wrens and skylarks and doves that flew above them should be able to land on them and rest awhile.

The vineyards gave way to an uncultivated field where wild iris and lavender, tamarisk with its tiny pink flowers, spear-like gladiolus, and orange-red poppies grew in profusion. Although it was late in the year, butterflies bobbled among the flowers and the droning of bees could be heard even over the rattle of the wagon. The day had advanced and the couple decided to stop next to the fragrant field and nibble from the basket the kitchen had prepared for them.

They were back on the road quickly enough and reached the out-skirts of Colossae as the sun had passed its zenith and was beginning to sink toward the horizon. Onesimus guided the horse through the streets he knew so well until he reached the walls that surrounded his childhood home.

He helped his bride down from the wagon and, calling at the entry into the courtyard, he was surprised to see a strange man approaching him. The man, taller and thinner than his father, was also quite a bit younger, Onesimus guessed him to be perhaps 35.

"Welcome, friends!" the stranger said. "What do you need that I may help you?"

"I am looking for the family who lived here four or five years ago. Have you any idea where they may have gone?"

The man considered for a few moments and then replied, "Sad case, that! I remember that the family had come on hard times. I traded my small farm, equipment, and my only slave to him for all this. The Goddess of Fortune had smiled on me and I felt it was time for my family to live as if she had.

"I believe they still live there and work the farm. If you would find them, turn right at the second corner and travel into the country. The farm you look for is on the right about half a league after you pass the mill. It has a good-sized cottage, a sheep cote, and three rows of grape vines. Good fortune to you on your travels!"

Onesimus and his bride thanked the man and climbed back into the wagon. Ephos was an old fella and not much inclined to hurry, so the trip would be stretched a little further than they had hoped but that was fine with them. It gave them a little more time to consider and discuss exactly how they would explain what they were doing there.

αω

CHAPTER TEN

Onesimus was surprised to realize how far the outer edges of Colossae had expanded in the time he had been gone.

Five years ago, a turn to the right where the man had indicated would have brought them into vast stretches of unpopulated land within a few minutes but now, it took another quarter of a league before they reached the weed-and-wildflower-strewn fields. A quarter of a league further and the grist mill appeared on their left. According to the man's directions it was a half-league from there to the farm where Onesimus parents were now living.

Shortly before they saw the buildings, they heard a man's voice shouting over the bleating of sheep, "No! I told you that you can't *do* it that way! You have to hold the ram by the horns so I can have a clear . . ."

As their wagon rattled to a stop, the man looked up. Recognizing the young man in the wagon, he dropped the bag of ointment he was using to doctor the cuts on the ram and ran toward the wagon, "Onesimus! My son! How I have prayed to the gods for this day to come! I searched for you at the slaver's market, but no one knew anything! I–," He stopped, stricken by the words that had just fallen from his lips.

"My son!" he said again in a whisper with tears springing to his eyes.

"My father!" Onesimus replied, grabbing Vincet, his father, in a bear hug and then his brother by the forearm. The years had not been kind to Vincet. The hard farm work he had been forced into these last few years had begun to bow his back and his hands were work-roughened whereas before they had been smooth and almost womanly in their softness. "My father! I am glad to see that you and Protos are well. And my mother? Is she within?" He grinned at Protos and set his feet in a wrestlers' stance as he pulled and pushed his brother's arm to knock him off balance and onto his rear. "I was always better at wrestling than you, brother!"

About that time, the door to the little cottage swung open and Portia, Onesimus' mother ran across the yard toward them. Without a pause, she seemed to launch herself directly for Onesimus, crying wordlessly and pummeling his shoulders. He stood and took the "beating" for several minutes before bending to embrace his mother.

"Son!" Vincet spoke quietly. "How can I make up to you . . . what I did was unforgiveable . . . I have begged the god's for a second chance . . . and now . . ."

Onesimus put his arm around his father's neck and moved him toward the house. "The gods you have begged have not brought this meeting about. They have nothing to do with me and I have nothing to do with them," he continued. "I have found peace and there is nothing you need to be forgiven for. In fact, I need to ask your forgiveness for the bitterness and anger I felt toward you. Please, Father, will you forgive me?"

Vincet looked at his younger son with amazement, "What? I need to forgive you?? Have you forgotten?"

Onesimus shook his head, "No. I've not forgotten . . . but what happened is much like the Hebrew Scriptures called the Torah that tell the story of a man named Joseph. Joseph was ambushed by his brothers and sold into slavery by them but in the end, because Joseph was in the position he was in, he was able to save not only his family but many other people who were enduring famine. Afterward, when he spoke to his brothers he said, "What you meant for evil, God meant for good," and that is what I'm telling you. There is a God who is above all other gods and He is a loving and kind God who wants the best for men and when men try to do evil to others, God takes that evil and turns it into something wonderful.

"You didn't mean evil when you were forced to sell me, but it wasn't a good thing, either. But I was sold to a man who knew this God of the Hebrews and he introduced me to Him as well. Later, yet, I met another man who taught me what I needed to know to understand this God.'

As they walked toward the cottage, Apollonia trailed along behind seemingly forgotten but when they had entered, Onesimus beckoned her forward and, wrapping his arm around her waist, introduced her around, "I would like you to meet Apollonia, my wife. Dear heart, this is my father, Vincet; my mother, Portia; and my older brother, Protos."

Surprised murmurs rose as Portia spoke, "O! So, you are free?"

Apollonia shook her head, "No. Our master believes that everyone deserves to be happy and does not refuse anyone the right to marry."

"But he will take your children and sell them away!"

"No, mother. That is not his way. He will allow them to grow up within the family," Onesimus replied. "In fact, he gave us the use of one of his olive wagons and a horse to make this trip just so we could talk to you about Yeshua and the God of the Hebrews."

They gathered in the shaded and cool salon and began telling each other about the events of their lives.

It was as Protos was telling of a moving day mishap that nearly cost him a leg that Onesimus began really *seeing* his mother. The raven hair was much grayer now and the amazingly amber eyes had a sadness about them he had never seen there before. Her slightly bushy eyebrows were closer together than he remembered and there was a faint vertical line between them.

Her porcelain skin had roughened. Small lines had begun to show at her neck and forehead and the creases running from her nose to her chin were deeper and more pronounced. Her soft and smooth hands had reddened from the harsh work that was now her duty although before it had always been done by the slaves. Even her voice had gotten rougher in these past few years.

He reached out and took her hands in his. "I am so sorry for your misfortune!" He said softly.

She patted his hand and smiled, "In truth, I am happier now than ever before," she whispered. "Vincet and I are much closer than we were when he was a man of substance. We talk as we never used to. Yes, I do miss my servants and my large house and all the rest . . . but the return of the man I married is worth all of it."

No one noticed that Apollonia was missing from the group and it wasn't until she came into the room bearing a huge tray of olives, dates, barley bread, olive oil and salt for dipping, and cheese that they realized she had been gone for quite some time.

Smiling, she said, "I thought you would all like to continue your visiting, so I went and found a meal for us. I hope that's acceptable."

Portia was a little taken aback but quickly recovered and graciously replied, "Of course! Thank you so much for your thoughtfulness."

Apollonia set the tray on a nearby table and everyone gathered around to collect their portions.

"Wait!" Onesimus said quietly. "It is the custom of those who follow the God of the Israelites to give thanks before they eat. May I?"

Vincet looked like he had swallowed a lit candle but nodded his head and Onesimus began.

"Lord and Father of the universe, it is with grateful hearts that we thank you for your protection on our journey and your blessings and mercies on this household. Thank you for bringing us safely to our family and bless everything that we say and do here this evening. In the name of Yeshua we ask all this, Amen."

"Who is this Yeshua and Lord and Father of the universe and, if He is so powerful why have we not heard of Him before?" Vincet asked when they were once again seated.

"Now, Father," Onesimus began, "I know you have heard of Mars Hill. The great center of philosophical debate."

Vincet nodded.

"Well, in that place, there is a great altar built that is dedicated to "The Unknown God". The man who taught me about the ways of Yeshua also went to Mars Hill and declared that this altar that was dedicated to the *Unknown God* was actually raised for this God whom we serve. The great philosophers of every age have known that there is some final authority. The ultimate force that started this world on its journey . . . some reason why we exist . . . how did we get here? Who is this God who is greater than all of Mount Olympus? It is, after all, impossible that a god who dwells in an earthly mountain like Olympus to actually be great enough to have created Mount Olympus, is it not? How can one who dwells on the earth have created the earth? Where did he dwell *before* the earth began?"

Vincet listened intently and then threw up his hands. "Enough! I am not interested in Philosophy! But *if* Yeshua is who you claim He is, and *if* you really know the "creator of the universe" then *I want to know Him too! The gods know* . . . HA! Did you hear that? The GODS know . . . HA! As far as my sacrifices and prayers and offerings have affected these miserable circumstances in which we now struggle *the gods I know, know nothing!*"

Onesimus suddenly realized that God had been preparing Vincet for this day for a long time. So he settled in and began to explain just exactly who God is; how he, Onesimus, knew this to be true; what had happened to him since his sale in the slaver's market; and why he wanted more than anything to see his father, mother, and brother come to know this God just as he did. It was late into the night before his father was satisfied that he had heard the truth and they all went to their pallets for their rest.

αω

CHAPTER ELEVEN

T he following day, Onesimus stayed to help his father doctor his
sheep and get them ready for shearing, which would take place
in a couple of weeks after all the sores they had collected in the
fields had time to heal. By noon he and Apollonia were on their way
back to Philemon's olive groves with a firm promise to return in time for
the shearing if their Master would allow them the time.

"Your mother is a grand lady!" Apollonia said shortly after their
departure. "She can't cook . . ." she patted her chest and made a face, "as
her midday meal has proven."

Onesimus laughed.

"But she *is* a grand lady," Apollonia concluded.

"Until their reversal of fortune, Mother never *had* to cook . . .
or clean, or help with chores, or . . . *anything*. There were slaves and
servants for everything. It has been terribly hard on her."

"I tried to show her a few quick tricks in the kitchen (such as cleaning as you cook) but I don't think she was very receptive," Philemon's
head cook said.

"Oh. She will have noticed everything you did and, next time we're
there, you will see that she has adopted most of your methods. She may
not yet be a wonderful cook, but she is very quick to learn and most
willing to do so. And, on behalf of my father and brother, I sincerely
thank you for your tutelage!"

Λ Ω

About halfway back, the rumbling and bumping of the unsprung wagon over the ruts and potholes of the road became more than the newlywed's backsides could endure so, without even a discussion, the wagon was drawn to the side of the road and they both climbed down. After a good stretch and a kiss or two as newlyweds tend to do, they climbed the bank beside the road and entered a field that was filled with wild grasses and wildflowers. Looking back at the wagon, they could see that their horse was enjoying the grasses as well, so they were content to wander through the meadow and collect a few prize specimens for their home. Apollonia found a cloth in the bed of the wagon and soaked it in a nearby stream, wrapping the stems of the flowers they had picked loosely within it in hopes of keeping the flowers alive.

Shortly, they wandered back to the wagon and, with a persistent butterfly flitting around Apollonia's head, started off again toward home.

"I told you your hair smells like flowers in springtime," Onesimus said as he reached out and touched her hair. "How do you make it smell that way?"

She just smiled and glanced his way, reaching out to place her hand in his.

The fields passed by; some filled with crops, others lying fallow with sheep grazing and wildflowers growing riotous within their borders. There were several orchards, none as large as Philemon's. Some held apples, some olives, one held both fig and pomegranate trees. They even saw a decent-sized vineyard shortly before they turned onto the road that led to Philemon's land and the little cottage they had already grown to love.

The way was narrow and the couple saw few fellow-travelers. Because it seemed so deserted, it wasn't long and Apollonia's head was on Onesimus' shoulder and his arm was wrapped protectively around her waist as he held both reins in his other hand. The rhythmic clopping of the horse's hooves, the swaying of the wagon, and the jingling of the harness's hardware began to lull the couple into a peaceful daze.

It was in this state the twosome entered the portion of road that entered a dark, cool wood. They had come almost to the halfway point . . . where they would no longer be *entering* the wood but would be *exiting* it instead . . . when they were startled to see two men standing in the narrow roadway before them. Without a way around, Onesimus was forced to draw the wagon to a stop. He tightened his grip on Apollonia and waited for what he knew the man would say next.

"Ho! My friend!" the burly, dark-haired man called out. "We've been waiting for you! I don't mind telling you we had almost gone home, but my brother and I are very hungry and very desperate. So, we waited a little longer than usual and finally, the gods be praised, they brought you to us! Now, if you will just hand over your traveling money and any food or other supplies you may have, we can all be on our way quickly."

During this verbose speech, the man's brother (if so he was), just stood there grinning and nodding giving the strong impression that he had less sense than the horse before them.

Onesimus spoke carefully, not wanting to give offense but also not wanting to be seen as weak or unable to protect his wife.

"Sirs. As you can see, we really don't have a lot with us. This was just a short trip to see my family in Colossae. We do have a basket with a few baked eggs and some olives back here and you are more than welcome to them, but this wagon and the horse belong to our master so there is nothing more we can give you."

"Not so!" the swarthy man exclaimed as he came around and took hold of Apollonia's arm. "You have this lovely piece of jewelry that I so admire. I will take this!"

Apollonia uttered a short scream of surprise and the man laughed roughly. When he opened his mouth, she could see his teeth were broken and black. She struggled against his grip and Onesimus dropped the reins and, holding tightly onto her, reached into the wagon bed and pulled out the small sword Philemon had sent with them for the trip. His youthful lessons on swordsmanship had always been the despair of his father but before the men could even see what he was holding, he had taken a swipe at the captors' ear and laid the point of the blade against his throat.

"You will release my wife immediately and apologize for frightening her!" he said with a firmness that startled even him.

The man did as he was told, tugged his forelock, and backed away. "My great apologies, madam!" Then he and his partner turned and plunged into the wood.

Apollonia turned shocked eyes to her husband. "Onesimus!" she said quietly. "Where did that come from?"

Onesimus could only shake his head in wonder. "I have no idea, beloved. No idea at all!"

αω

CHAPTER TWELVE

One week after his return Onesimus found himself deep into the season's final books, arguing with a column that simply did not add up no matter what he did.

Struggling to keep his temper, he laid the stylus down on his desk and growled quietly. Propping his elbows on the desk and his head on his hands, he just sat there, staring at the numbers.

If ten amphorae of olive oil was traded at five denarii each for three bolts of linen at seven denarii each and a new axe-head at ten denarii, then that should leave nineteen denarii's worth of goods or coin still owing to us, but for some reason, I keep coming up with nine denarii in coin!

"Now what is going on?"

He hadn't even realized he was speaking aloud until he felt that rock-like paw of Philemon land on his shoulder.

"What is what going on?" Philemon asked as he perused the figures before him. "OH! Onesimus! I am so sorry!" he said with a grin on his face. "You're missing ten denarii's worth of goods and services or coin I see. I forgot to tell you. That ten denarii was added to an offering being sent to the Jerusalem church to feed the brothers in need there."

Onesimus labored to keep his eyes from rolling as he picked up his stylus. He took in a deep breath and held it so he wouldn't embarrass himself with a huge sigh.

"Ahh . . . put your stylus down, Onesimus. I need to speak with you and Apollonia; and I want all your attention. Gather your wife and come meet me in your cottage," Philemon said as he started for the door.

A small knot formed in Onesimus' chest as he stood from his stool and followed Philemon out the door. So many possibilities, good and bad, lay before him but, knowing his Master the way he did, he believed this meeting would bring good news.

Trying not to alarm Apollonia, Onesimus came to the door of the kitchen and called for her to join him.

"You know I can't leave right now. I have the evening meal to tend to and . . ."

"You need to come now, dearest," Onesimus interrupted. "Is there no one who can watch the cookery for you?"

Apollonia wrinkled her brow and then nodded. "All right. Casta can handle it. Casta! See to the cooking while I'm absent. I won't be long."

"The master wants to see us. He says he has something to say and he needs us to meet him at our cottage," Onesimus tried to make his voice light because he didn't wish to worry his wife, but in spite of the trust he held in his Master, he remembered all too well how "talks" between master and slave usually went in his childhood home. He tried to convince himself that the words "selling" and "new master" wouldn't come up in the conversation, but he remembered.

As they came up to the cabin, Philemon stood from the porch and followed them into the humble cottage they called home.

"This is *your* home. Seat yourselves," the master said.

After they were seated Philemon began to speak.

"You both have done such a good job for me and I have been blessed to have you as a part of my family. I want you to know that I appreciate all you do and would like to keep you on here," he continued as the knot of dread in Onesimus' breast continued to grow. "But I have been considering what Paulus said to me when he sent you home to me, Onesimus."

He's going to send me off to serve Paul! Onesimus thought. *Will he send Apollonia, too?* He looked at his beloved in dismay and secretly reached out to take her hand.

"He wrote that he wanted me to receive you as I would receive him, and I am ashamed to say I did no such thing. To imagine Paulus coming here and being put to work as a slave! What a shameful thing to do! So! SO!" Philemon stood abruptly and began to pace. "I can no longer hold you as slaves! I must release you as soon as arrangements can be made."

Apollonia, who had grown gray and pale as Philemon talked about Paulus, slid her eyes sideways to watch Onesimus' reaction to what was being said. At the same time, Onesimus' eyes slid sideways and met hers.

There was silence in the cottage and Philemon stood and stared at them, awaiting their reaction. At first, he just looked at them, then his eyebrows bounced upward and he held out his hands, palms up in a questioning manner as he shook his head.

"What . . ." Onesimus' voice came out hoarse, so he cleared his throat and tried again, "What does this mean? How long do we have before we need to leave?"

"Leave? *Leave?*" Philemon almost roared. "Why, I hope you *never* leave! I don't want you to stop working here. I just can't keep you as slaves! I have, in fact, come to the conclusion that I cannot in good conscience hold any of my Christian brothers and sisters as slaves. I will, over the next several months be working out a plan with your help to begin paying all the Christians who work for me. Of course, their housing and meals will be part of what they earn but beyond that, they (you first) will be given a small payment of cash so they can work for me and pay their own way. Not only will you be expected to continue to work for me, you will even be given the chance to purchase this cottage since Quintin has chosen to build another cottage on the grounds when he is ready to marry.

"This evening, after the evening meal, come to the main house and I will give you both your papers of manumission. If you do not wish to buy it, this house is yours to use as long as you work for this family. That will be part of your wages. If the other slaves question you, feel free to tell them the truth, that over the next few months all Christian slaves who work for me will be freed and begin receiving wages as well as their room and board. If anyone who is not a Christian asks, tell them that as soon as they accept Christ and his sacrifice that may be theirs, when their lives bear the fruits of Christianity, they, too will be freed.

"Because I know this is a shock, I would suggest you stay here and spend a little time discussing this before you go back to work," with that parting sentence, Philemon left the young couple, sitting in utter confusion, and went back to the olive press where he collapsed onto his stool, swiped the perspiration from his brow, and leaned heavily on his elbow as he considered all the ramifications of what he had just done

While Philemon was considering what kind of new expenses his decision would bring to his business, Onesimus and Apollonia were discussing what this meant for them. How would the other slaves respond when they heard the news? Would they find themselves in some sort of no-man's land half-way between slave and servant? Would they still have friends among the unsaved slaves, or would the resentment make it impossible to fellowship with them?

Onesimus returned to the olive press after the couples' speculations ended up with the decision to just 'wait and see' what would transpire. He really wanted to talk with the Master but Marcus and Antitus, were in the room getting instructions for the winter's chores so he had to curb his desires until they were gone. While he waited, he set about reconciling that ten denarii difference in the books, putting it down as a debt paid to the Jerusalem church and how true that was! He reflected to himself. If it weren't for the faithful at Jerusalem who followed the instructions of Yeshua, neither Philemon nor any other Gentiles would have heard of Yeshua as anyone more important than the other groups who planned insurrection against the Romans. Yes . . . Philemon and all Gentile Christians owed a great debt to the Jerusalem church.

As soon as his two fellow-slaves had departed to make estimates of the amount of repairs needed to the pens and corrals, Onesimus approached Philemon who was staring into space as if he had just heard some shocking news.

"Master?"

Philemon gave a start and turned to look at Onesimus, "Oh! I will shortly not be your master, Onesimus," Philemon said. "I know it may take some getting used to, so I would suggest you begin practicing to just call me 'Sir'."

"Sir," Onesimus said. It really wasn't too hard. He had called his father *Agha* for most of his life and, until he was sold to Philemon, he had never had to call anyone *Affendis* except the occasional Senator or Praetor he might be introduced to. He paused and took a deep breath.

"Sir, I just wanted to thank you for this chance! Apollonia and I will serve—mmm—work for you—as hard as ever we did . . ."

Philemon waved his hand. "I know you will. You are a good man and my brother, and you deserve your freedom."

Onesimus spoke again, "Will you speak of this at this Lord's Day meeting tomorrow?"

Philemon's brow creased in concentration.

"Well, now. It's a difficult thing to do," he said. "One isn't to trumpet one's good deeds so there is that to consider . . . however, YOU need to be known as a free man rather than my slave! On top of that is the difficulty of communicating this idea to other slave-owners in the Body without stirring discontent in the slaves who are present. I certainly don't want anyone to think I'm trying to say all slave-owners need to do this, or that because I've decided to do this everyone else has to! "

"While that is all true . . . *sir* . . . it is an example that others might be influenced to do."

"True. But imagine the foment that this could stir among the other slaves that attend the Lord's Day services! I think that instead of announcing what has been done, instead I may speak of the Christian slave as a brother in general. Then I will personally talk with different slave owners and tell them what we have done," Philemon sat pondering for a moment and then nodded decisively. "Yes. That is the way to handle it. But . . . tonight at dinner I will come to the men's slave quarters and tell them what we are doing. You and Apollonia can be there to eat so we will all be together. "You were wise to bring this up so we could work out a few of the details," Philemon said as he turned back to his work.

Λ Ω

It was unusual for married slaves to appear at the door of the men's quarters for the evening meal. Usually, they enjoyed their own meals in their own quarters, taking appropriate amounts from the meals provided for the single men and women. In fact, it was so unusual that Justin stood in the doorway to the men's quarters blinking out at Onesimus and Apollonia.

"Well, Justin! May we come in? Or are we *personae non grata* here?" Onesimus said with a grin.

Still, Justin just tilted his head to the left and looked at them for a second. It was as if he had never seen these people before . . . until a booming voice from the shadows made him jump and open the door wide, "Come, come, Justin! Let the poor man and his wife in for a good meal!"

Philemon hurried up and followed the couple into the room.

"Are we on time?" he asked.

"Oh! Yes Master! On time, indeed!" Justin replied.

This time it was Justin that felt the rock that was Philemon's hand descend onto his shoulder. "Good, Good! We brought our own trenchers, so move down a bit so we may have seats because we have important news to talk over when we are all settled and eating."

If Justin was nonplussed when he saw Onesimus and Apollonia at the door, he was even more confused when the Master came in and sat down beside his slaves as if to eat with them. Even so, Justin picked up his routine as he did every night and spoke to those gathered, "Let us give thanks to the Lord for the blessings of the good home, good food, and good treatment we enjoy," he said and, lifting up his hands he prayed, "Father of all mankind and creator of all good things, we praise your name for your goodness to us. You have given us health and shelter and a good master to work for and we thank you. Bless this bounty that you have provided and keep us ever aware of the gratitude we owe you. In the name of our savior, Yeshua we pray. Amen."

The bowls and platters were passed around the table. The wines were poured and everyone began to eat. As the serving dishes settled once more to the table and the workers began to concentrate on the food, Philemon spoke.

"Onesimus, Apollonia, and I are here with an announcement . . ." here he was interrupted as the people around the table began to titter and whisper. Most obviously thought the announcement was about an impending addition (although the master had never found it necessary to make any other such announcement). "Haarrrumph!" he continued. "There are changes coming to the olive groves and those who work here."

He has certainly gotten everyone's attention now! Onesimus thought. Under cover of the table, Apollonia took his hand in hers. Hers was cold with nerves and shook just a little. He looked at her and gazed steadily into her eyes until he felt her hand relax and saw her shoulders drop. He smiled as she told him with her eyes that he was her strength.

"Since Onesimus' return I have been thinking about something our friend Paulus wrote in the letter he sent with Onesimus. I have recently come to some conclusions and want to let you know because what I have decided affects every one of you."

Now, the whispers and titters arose again, but died quickly when they realized there was a lot more to come.

Philemon continued, "Paulus told me to receive Onesimus back to myself as a brother as I would receive Paulus himself. I have realized that I have not yet done that. How can I say I have since I would never think of putting Paulus in chains? Expecting *him* to serve *me*? I could not . . . I cannot. So, I am manumitting both Onesimus and Apollonia right now." With this he pulled two scrolls from under his cloak and handed them with a smile to the now *former* slaves.

The table erupted in gasps and questions and among the other noises, a smattering of applause and a few even began sobbing.

Philemon held up his hands and spoke again, "I have decided that I can no longer hold my Christian brothers and sisters as slaves so those of you who name the Name will also be manumitted over the next few weeks and months. It will take this amount of time to have the proper papers written up. For those of you who are not believers, please understand that you can accept Yeshua at any time and you, too, will be freed but you need to keep in mind that we have already heard of people being killed for the sake of the Gospel and I have no doubt that more persecution is at hand. You must accept Yeshua's salvation, understanding that there is no question that many Christians will be persecuted, and understanding that your behavior and life must reflect your decision. Without that evidence, I will not take your word that you have converted.

"Outside of Onesimus and Apollonia, all manumissions will be distributed one or two at a time over the next few weeks, in the order in which you came to us. Those who have been here the longest will be freed first, families will be freed together according to the arrival of the longest service. I hope that you will all stay with us as servants. You will still be provided room and meals as part of your pay and you will be given some money as well. Well, that's what I had to say. Why don't we go ahead and enjoy this wonderful food?"

With that, he began to eat and soon hunger overcame curiosity, wonder, and pique that were the prevailing emotions at the table. Then, those who were around him took up their meals as well.

αω

CHAPTER THIRTEEN

Onesimus lay beside Apollonia and stared into the darkness. A smear of light from the full moon shone through the open window and blazed a trail straight to the small table on the other side of the room. On that table lay the documents that drew Onesimus's thoughts and held his eyes open. In the light from the window, the scrolls almost seemed to glow with their own light.

How long had he dreamed of this day? How long had he struggled to become submitted to God's will that he be a slave? How long had he prayed that someday—maybe on the day the Master died—he would be set free? Free to do as he chose! To stay or go! To earn his own money and eat his own bread that he had earned by his own labor and paid for with money from *his own purse*!

It was important to acknowledge that Philemon was a good Master. He kept his slaves quartered and clothed and fed not just adequately but with generosity. Onesimus had heard him say many times, "If your slaves are dressed in rags and underfed it is a clear indication that your soul is dressed in rags and underfed!" Even so, whether an owner was a good Master or an evil Master, he was still a Master and his slaves were still obliged to give him allegiance. But *now*—both he and his beautiful Apollonia were free! They could go or stay. They could work for anyone they chose, or they could set up a business of their own. Their bodies were their own and their souls belonged to no one but Yeshua.

Yet, Onesimus thought. *The Master has been so good to us through the years it is hard to imagine leaving him.* He thought back to the early days: the first time he'd seen the white walls of the house and olive press gleaming in the sun, the great relief he felt when Philemon told him he would be working at accounting rather than pounding olive trees, the amazement he felt the first time he looked into Apollonia's beautiful gray eyes.

He remembered the first time he tasted the decent wine at the supper table and sat amazed comparing it to the *Posca* (near-vinegar wine) his parents supplied for their slaves.

He recalled the gut-wrenching fear that had grabbed him when he was told there were amphorae of oil missing and he couldn't account for them anywhere. His fear that he would be beaten if he couldn't explain the loss just as his father would beat his slaves. Even if Philemon chose to kill him on the spot, the Master would be perfectly justified according to the law. So he ran. He stole a purse of money and ran all the way from the olive grove outside Colossae to the great city of Rome and into the arms of Yeshua!

The adventures he had and the people he met had been frightening and funny, infuriating and fascinating and the memories of those days were covered in a golden haze of joy that it had all come down to Yeshua dragging him with love and vigor to a place where he could finally find out what he needed to do!

If it hadn't been for Philemon and the love and self-control he displayed to everyone, Onesimus would still be lost in the darkness of bitterness and despair. There was no reason why he and his wife should leave right now. Perhaps another day but for now they would stay right where they were. He nodded to himself and just as the moonlight was leaving the window, Onesimus' eyes drifted shut and he slept.

Λ Ω

His nose twitched. What? Who? **twitch** mmmm! Smells wonderful! What is . . . ? He sat up and swung his feet over the side of the bed.

"Husband! I wondered if you would ever join me! Quintin and some friends went fishing yesterday and they brought back enough fish that he gave some to us. I thought I would make a celebration breakfast of roasted fish and fresh barley bread!" Apollonia sounded so pleased with herself and excited Onesimus didn't have the heart to tell her he really didn't like fish, so he sat down and, after offering a prayer, began to eat . . . and was amazed!

This was wonderful! It had a crunchy crust and a hint of almonds to it. The flavor was mild and the flesh was flaky and almost sweet.

"Wife!" he exclaimed, "You are a genius with a fire! I've never cared for fish, but you have created a fish dish I am glad to say is delicious!" He jumped from his seat, grabbed Apollonia around the waist, and began to make foolish kissing sounds as he chased her ears and she laughed and kept moving her head to keep them out of his reach.

"Husband! Now stop!" She said through her laughter. "We both have to prove that we can be responsible free people! We have to show up to our work on time!"

He stopped and stared at her, "Free people!" He repeated. "Free people. By all means we MUST show up on time because WE ARE FREE PEOPLE!" He released her and danced around the cabin, picking up his clothing and sandals and setting them on the bed while he washed up and began dressing. As he pulled on his second sandal he glanced around the room. "Where are they?"

"I put them on the top of the cupboard where they would be safe."

Rising and placing his hand on the indicated furniture, he felt the small scrolls and nodded. "Very wise! They are not in constant sight and not in danger of accidental damage and yet they are available if we need them. I don't know what I ever did without you!" and with that, he lunged at her again and she deftly scooted away.

Then, patting his cheek, she smiled up at him, "Come, husband. It's time to work," and together they stepped through the door and started across the field toward their jobs.

αω

CHAPTER FOURTEEN

Over the next few weeks Philemon was true to his word and began releasing his Christian brothers and sisters from bondage until they all carried small scrolls with them whenever they left the grounds to prove they were free men and women.

Six non-Christians came to him and either tried to pretend to conversion or else tried to argue that if it was wrong to hold Christian slaves it was just as wrong to hold non-Christian slaves but Philemon held his ground, explaining to each that holding a Christian in chains was, to a Christian master, the same thing as enslaving his or her own sibling because Christian masters and Christian slaves were a part of the same family.

The six who pretended to conversion were "put to the test". Philemon explained the common process to each of them by saying that first they needed to spend two years learning about their new faith. Then they needed to be baptized and after they were baptized they could be considered full members of the church and a Christian brother or sister. Four actually passed the test and began their lessons while the other two shook their heads and walked away deeming the two-years of teaching to be excessive although all Christian converts underwent the same teaching cycle.

Some, though, refused to convert because of their own sense of integrity and although sorrowed by their obstinacy, Philemon admired these men and women for their honesty.

By the beginning of the olive harvest, Philemon had freed nine of his fifteen slaves and only two had left his groves to return to their homes in other lands. He was pleased to find that the six slaves and seven workers he still had had done their work as thoroughly as if all fifteen were still there.

While the freeing of nine slaves caused a small brouhaha around Philemon's place, the act didn't reach full tempest response until the householders that worshipped together at his home overheard their own slaves discussing the situation with Philemon's slaves!

How could Philemon act so irresponsibly? They asked. *Didn't he realize that his actions were going to stir up the slaves at these other homes? How were they supposed to respond when their own slaves began to demand their freedom? It was bad enough that Philemon had earlier set such a generous example concerning the treatment of slaves . . . now he was stirring up rebellion among them!*

That Lord's Day, as people were waiting to break their fast, Philemon took Onesimus aside.

"I will need your advice, my friend," he said quietly. "There are both angry owners and slaves who are on the verge of rebellion in this crowd."

"We need to say something before we take the Lord's Supper!" Onesimus replied. "It is necessary that a spirit of forgiveness becomes the spirit of this group or there will be some who eat and drink unworthily."

Nodding, Philemon moved toward the tables to his accustomed place.

"Brothers, I come before you with a deep concern in my heart," he began. "It has become known that I have freed many of my slaves and it has caused strife and dissention among the owners and slaves who worship here."

Heads began nodding and owners looked at one another with raised eyebrows.

Slaves who had gathered together by themselves rather than mingling as they had always done before, quieted so they could hear what was being said.

"I am so sorry that my actions have stirred trouble for you all and I want to explain why I chose to free my slaves," Philemon continued.

"When my runaway slave, Onesimus, returned to me he brought with him a letter from our dear brother Paulus. In that letter, Paulus urged me to accept Onesimus as I would accept Paulus himself and I thought I had done that. Even so, the Lord began to speak to me. He told me that for me holding a Christian brother as a slave was like holding my *own* brother in chains. He asked me if I would put Paulus in chains when he came for a visit. He urged me to do right by Onesimus…and this led me to wonder if it was right to hold *other* of my Christian brothers and sisters as slaves.

"I finally came to the conclusion that, for me, it was *not* right. That does not mean it is not right *for you*. Every man must respond as God leads him. I have freed those slaves who have proven to be followers of Christ Jesus because *I* must see them as my brothers and sisters . . . not my property.

"At the same time, I urge you all to listen to the voice of God leading you to deeper truths. I urge all the slaves now present to bear with your masters in peace. Paulus has urged you to treat your masters with respect and give thanks to God for the Godly men and women who own you. You could have it far worse than to serve a man or woman of God.

"Those of you who bear ill will toward me, your masters, or any other person, I urge you to clear up those ungodly feelings and return to the straight path before you partake of the Lord's supper today. Now let us break our fast."

When grace was completed, all those who worshipped together ate together with the exception of a few people (slave and master) who found quiet places to wrestle with what they had heard and come to some sort of decision concerning that message.

αω

CHAPTER FIFTEEN

Onesimus," Philemon called from across the olive press floor. "I've had a letter and thought you might like to see it." He held the letter out toward the former slave and continued, "I've hesitated to show this to you, because I don't want to lose your skills at harvest, but I can't hold out any longer."

Slipping from his stool, Onesimus crossed the room and took the extended missive.

To Philemon my dear Brother in Christ, Greetings, it began.

I have been traveling through the region and have found there a new church which is in need of closer supervision than I am able to provide at this time.

I have heard of your generous gift of freedom to your Christian brothers and sisters in chains and was interested to know if any of those men and women who have benefitted thus might be willing to assist this church with their spiritual health.

Most specifically, I have in mind Onesimus and his new wife, Apollonia. They would still work for you for their livelihood but would spend part of their time teaching the new believers who need further instruction before being baptized into the church. I would suggest they could do this with a weekly catechetical session on the Seventh Day.

One of the new believers, Valerius, has offered his own home in Laodicea as a possible place to hold this class.

I know you have a great deal of work for Onesimus, but I am certain you can find a way to help us in this endeavor.

I look forward to hearing from you AND from Onesimus
soon about this matter and urge you to pray diligently concerning
it before you reply.
    May the light of Christ be with you,

    Tarchus

Onesimus handed the message back to Philemon and reached across his body with his right arm to scratch his left elbow. His look of puzzlement and surprise struck Philemon as funny and he began to grin and then chuckle.

"Well, boy, what think you?" he boomed. "Could you do in five days what you have been doing in six? Are you smart enough to teach others?" He softened his voice and said gently, "Will you pray about this? I am more than willing to let you help if you feel this is God's will for you."

Shaking his head slightly, Onesimus replied, "I honestly don't know. I'm surprised that Tarchus would even think of a former slave for such a position but . . ." his voice faded off and he stood there, regarding Philemon solemnly. "You know, when Protos and I were boys we would play school and I always had to be the teacher. He would get so mad at me because I expected the answers he gave to be correct and he would shout, 'We're only playing here! You aren't my teacher so stop CORRECTING me!'" Onesimus chuckled at the memory. "But I need to be certain this is what God wants, so—yes. I will pray about this."

Taking a deep breath of olive-scented air, he returned to his accounting books and took up his quill as Philemon secretly smiled and nodded his head. He had been praying about this since he had gotten the letter and he knew what the answer would be. But that was all right. When Onesimus had come to his decision, he would ask him to train Quintin in the ins and outs of accounting so that, in a few years, when Onesimus moved from Catechist to some other position within the church there would be no gap in his accounting books and he would not have to return to doing his own bookkeeping.

He would miss Onesimus when he was gone, but he knew there were other duties that his former slave was destined to perform for Christ and with that he was content.

αω

CHAPTER SIXTEEN

Onesimus kept his own counsel for several days, pondering quietly about the request. To be quite honest, he wasn't sure he was up to the task of teaching others about The Way. It was a great responsibility and the thought that something he said might turn someone into the wrong path struck great fear within him. Finally, he arrived at the point where he began to do more than just contemplating the idea and began praying about it.

Apollonia, in the meantime, could see that her sweetheart was greatly absorbed in something he was mulling over but she, like the wise woman she was, said nothing. She only continued to keep warm meals on the table and a warm heart in the home. She, too, began praying and although she didn't know what she was praying about, she knew the Holy Spirit did know and would guide her prayers aright.

After a week of mutual but loving silence, Apollonia was not surprised when her husband began to roll around on their bed until she thought she would end up on the floor. But although he always came within inches of crowding her out, he would then turn the other way and continued his rotating travels to the far side of the bed. She had been married to him long enough by now to recognize the signs that God was sending him a dream that would give him the final answer to his prayer so she settled into sleep knowing she would hear about his dream as soon as he could make sense of God's message.

Two days later Apollonia came in one evening carrying a large bowl of lamb stew and a loaf of crusty rye bread from the Master's kitchen. Because of Philemon's generosity, she never had to cook at home. Any time she wished she could simply help herself to her day's work and she did so about once a week. Today was that day and she hurried to set the table as Onesimus looked up from repairing his sandal and sniffed loudly.

"Mmmm! Something smells like lamb stew!" he declared loudly. "I am so glad you brought dinner home tonight because I have a dream to tell you and an important decision to make. Because you are now my wife it is one we must make together."

His bride smiled with relief. The waiting was over. Now Onesimus would tell her what they had been praying about, what his dream was about and what they were deciding!

"I need to let you know right away that, if I do this thing, I will be traveling into Laodicea every seventh day. I will leave early in the morning and stay until the sixth hour and return in the evening," Onesimus began. "Philemon has had a letter requesting that he send someone to teach a group of new believers so they do not err. The writer even suggested me . . . but I was not sure I could do this thing until God sent me a dream the other night."

Apollonia nodded and sat down beside Onesimus, prepared to hear the dream.

"In this dream, I was working on Philemon's books but every time I added a column of numbers, the totals were either wrong or would just disappear from the page! I was so frustrated that I felt as if nothing I did was worth anything. It seemed I had been adding this same column of numbers over and over for hours when finally I threw down my quill and let out a shout of disgust. Just then, an older man appeared before me in shining white robes but, even as I watched the robes began to collect dirt as if the man was rubbing filth on them yet, at the same time, he was weeping and calling to me saying, 'Come quickly and help me understand what to do! Teach me to keep my robes white. We need you so badly!'"

Onesimus had been looking at the surface of the table but looked up into Apollonia's beautiful face. "I think I may be able help them, but I'm hesitant to leave you every week!"

"You are a well-educated man and spent almost *two whole years* with Paulus learning about The Way! There is no reason why you can't do this," Apollonia said. Along with this, perhaps you won't need to leave me. After all, the wives of those men in Laodicea also need to learn how to be Godly wives. Perhaps Philemon would be willing to allow me to go as well. There are a couple of capable cooks that can take over the duties for the household while we're gone. Whether I am with you or not, though, I know you must do this. Why don't we approach Philemon to see if we could do this together? My only other concern is how much extra work will your one-day teaching in Laodicea add to your duties here?"

Onesimus smiled and reached out to take the busiest hands he'd ever touched. "Not that much. Philemon is a good man. He told me the other day that, if I decide to do this he will set Quintin to watch me and ask questions so he can help with the Saturday work. If you really would like to work with me, I think Philemon will consider it, but I am a little fearful, my love. If I do this it is a great responsibility. I never would want to set a student's course the least bit off! And yet, I am excited as well. If I choose this path . . ."

His wife smiled and patted his whiskery cheek with one of those busy hands. "Husband! You know you want to do this! And you know that it is God that is calling you to it. Don't make Philemon wait any longer for his answer . . . nor delay in writing to Tarchus. It will take some time to get things arranged here, so you had best do it quickly."

The amazed husband stared in wonderment at his beautiful helpmate. *She knows exactly what to say to encourage me,* he thought as he cleared the table and began to heat water to clean the after-dinner clutter.

αω

CHAPTER SEVENTEEN

O nesimus, A Servant of the Most High God, to Tarchus his
fellow-laborer,
    When first I was given your letter I struggled with the idea
that I might be called upon to pass the teachings of Petros, Paulus,
Johannan and other of the venerable Apostles of the church.
Who was I to presume to teach others when I was, only a few
years before, in the same position these new believers now find
themselves in? It was with great reluctance, and not a few doubts
about this calling that I undertook to pray about your call.
    It wasn't until I reread your missive that I realized you
had requested both me and my wife for this blessing. When
I approached Philemon he was more than willing to allow us
both to catechize your Laodicean body. So, we believe that we
will be able to begin our lessons within a fortnight or as soon as
you can arrange to meet with us and your friend, Valerius we
will begin.

    I continue to be your brother in Christ, Onesimus.

It was midweek and Quintin had been sitting beside Onesimus watching
and listening since before Lord's Day. The teacher was much encouraged
to realize that Quintin was beginning not only to understand how the
system worked but was beginning to ask questions when he wasn't clear
on something.

    Onesimus' old tutor used to tell him, "When you know enough to
ask questions, you're beginning to understand."

"Hello?" the question came from the entrance to the olive press. "We're looking for Philemon and his bookkeeper. Are you they?"

Onesimus turned on his stool and nodded. "I am Onesimus. Philemon has gone to visit his mother-in-law across the meadow. May I ask who . . . ?"

"I am Tarchus and this is Valerius. He was so eager to meet the man who will help the body in Laodicea that I couldn't persuade him to write a letter and await your response . . . and, to be completely fair, I was pretty eager, too."

Onesimus capped his ink bottles, nodded at Quintin in dismissal, and walked across the press's floor, stepping outside with the two men. He was not the least surprised to see that Valerius was the man he had seen in his dream. He was half-a-head shorter than Onesimus and had several scars on his face and arms. His brown eyes and hair and his excited countenance were so average, Onesimus was afraid that if he turned away for a moment and then turned back, he wouldn't remember who Valerius was.

Tarchus, on the other hand was another like Philemon. Tall . . . his completely bald head hovered about two heads above Onesimus and he was large...all over, large. His hand, when he saluted the man he'd come to see, could have completely covered Onesimus' face if he had wanted to. While much of his size was muscle there was a bit of over-indulgence involved as well. Even so, it was clear the man was strong and healthy and full of God's joy.

"I know you have come a distance and would like to get down to business with Philemon and me, so why don't we take a walk and find my employer?" The designation of Philemon as Onesimus' employer certainly wasn't necessary but there was nothing Onesimus liked better lately than to clarify his standing with his former Master . . . for no other reason than it allowed him to declare his freedom once again.

The trio set off across the meadow where wildflowers sprouted and bumblebees bumbled and butterflies flittered between the blossoms. The weeds and grasses made ruffling, rattling sounds as they brushed the legs of the men passing through them and the heat of the sun was suddenly cooled a bit by large, heavy clouds passing in front of it. Onesimus was careful to steer the men close to a patch of wild lavender that had taken root in the southwest quadrant of the meadow. The only reason the former slave did this was because the strong and pleasant odor of the plants reminded him of the field of lavender he had discovered during his desperate run and the peace of heart he had found a few weeks after he had spied it.

Approaching the cottage, Onesimus called out to those inside, "Hail the Cot! Brother Philemon, we have sojourners who have come from Laodicea! Are you free to meet them?"

The door flew open and both Philemon (who knew who the visitors must be) and his mother-in-law, Rhais, (who had no idea) stepped onto the porch.

"Ho and welcome!" Philemon called. "I am guessing that these must be Valerius and Tarchus but I'll be honest and confess I have no idea who is whom!" He stepped down from the porch as Tarchus stepped forward.

"I am Tarchus of Sardis and this is Valerius. We have come so that we can settle all the questions about Onesimus' coming to Laodicea to tutor the new church there," came the reply. "I understand this is your mother-in-law." Tarchus and Valerius both bowed deeply toward the tall and dignified woman standing near the open door to her cottage.

"Yes. This is Rhais. Mother Rhais, as you have heard, these are two men who have asked that Onesimus be allowed to travel to Laodicea every Seventh Day." At Rhais' nod, Philemon continued, "There is a new church growing there but they need a teacher who can guide them in the ways of the Lord. Tarchus sent a missive requesting the help of Onesimus and, since Onesimus has studied under Paulus himself, we have come to believe that this is what God would have us do. Quintin has been learning bookkeeping from Onesimus and I believe he will be able to take over Onesimus' Seventh Day work by next week. Would that be acceptable to you?" He had been facing Rhais on her doorstep but now turned to look at the trio who was standing on the packed dirt walkway leading to the cottage.

Without even a thought, a glance toward one another, or a murmured word, the three found themselves nodding and smiling at Rhais, at Philemon and even at one another.

Leave it to Philemon to get down to business and settle all questions with a single sentence! Onesimus thought wryly.

"Onesimus," Rhais spoke quietly but with authority. "I have a small pony cart that Quintin and Blandina used to use but which they have grown to believe is too undignified for them. If you would like you may use that for your travels. Would that be acceptable to you, Philemon?"

"Wonderful! I was wondering if there was an alternative to having them use one of those hulking olive wagons for the journey!" Philemon replied with a smile. "We will take it up to the wagon shed and ask the wheelwright to check it over and ensure its soundness for the trip. Thank you, Mother Rhais!"

After polite fare-thee-wells, the four men stepped behind the cottage and took hold of the little two-wheeled cart, dragging it up to the shed where all repairs on wagons were done. After Philemon had given instructions to his wheelwright, the men continued to the house where a fine midday meal had been laid out. There they enjoyed a fine repast and then said their good-byes, knowing that they would see Onesimus the Seventh Day following this coming Lord's Day.

αω

CHAPTER EIGHTEEN

B ack . . . back . . . back!" Onesimus murmured encouragingly to the little dapple-gray mare that would carry him and his bride to Laodicea. He backed her between the traces of the pony cart and slipped the breast strap over her head. Fastening the martingale and other lines to the appropriate fixtures, he patted and stroked little Poppy as he worked, talking soothingly to her, and helping her to trust what he was doing.

After she was harnessed and ready to go, he took a carrot from his pocket and held it out to her on his upturned palm. She nuzzled his hand and then picked the vegetable from his hand and chomped it down. While she was busy with her treat, Onesimus stepped over to the door of his cottage and called quietly, "Apollonia, time to go!"

She came to the door still fastening her veil in place. "Yes, dear. If you will take this basket I will be right there."

Onesimus shook his head and rolled his eyes. "Wife! You know our midday meal is going to be provided for us. Why are you . . ."

"One doesn't show up at another's home for a meal without providing a few special things to add delight to it, husband! It is a good thing you have me with you to teach you the finer points of etiquette." She laughed as she seated herself in the cart and settled the basket upon her lap.

Casting his mind back to his boyhood, he remembered his mother always took a basket with them when they traveled to another's home for a meal. "So *that* is why mother always took food with her to their homes. I thought she was just making certain she had something she liked in case she didn't like what was served!" he laughed.

Apollonia looked appalled as she stared at her dearest love. "What an awful thing to think about your own mother! . . . Besides," she said archly, "perhaps I was thinking they might serve fish, and I know how you *love* the harvest of the sea!"

Onesimus glanced at her as he popped the reins lightly to keep Poppy moving, "I was fine with fish . . . until I spent all that time aboard the *Swan* eating hard tack and salted or smoked fish! Something about eating food that tastes of nothing but wood smoke and salt makes one a little weary of that food." He smiled as he reached out and adjusted his wife's veil a little—not that it needed adjusting. He just enjoyed allowing his hand to brush across her lovely auburn waves.

She pulled her head back a little and tilted it to the right, "Now, if you knock my veil sideways I'm never going to forgive you," she laughed.

Tender smiles and laughter, light conversation and more weighty discussion, hugs and even a stolen kiss or two were the shared moments of that first ride into Laodicea that set the pattern for every Seventh Day trip after that.

ΛΩ

"Onesimus is here!" Valerius shouted from the doorstep as he went to meet the little pony cart in his yard.

Seven men came from the house, stomping down the steps and crossing the yard with smiles wreathing their faces. Onesimus clasped hands with each man, hand near elbow, forearms together as each was introduced by Valerius; "Plutarchus, Serenus, Heron, Heraclides, Ponticus, Sanctus, and Martial."

When each had greeted their teacher with great joy, they returned to the house, where Onesimus brought laughter to the room by saying, "While you can remember my name . . . after all, it is the same for each of you . . . *I* have to remember *eight* names, so please be tolerant of my mistakes."

While all this was going on, Apollonia was busy becoming acquainted with the five women who had remained on the doorstep while their husbands greeted their new catechist. With the women were also three young girls. Two were the daughters of Plutarchus and his wife, Martina. The third young girl was betrothed to Heron and would be married to him before the year was gone.

Names of all the women were exchanged, but again, it was understood that it would take time for all the names to be remembered and applied to the proper faces.

The only woman Apollonia was certain she would never forget was Marcella, wife of Sanctus who had only come to the faith within the fortnight. Apollonia struggled to keep her countenance neutral as she asked Sanctus about the fresh black eye and a large bruise on her wrist and Marcella's reply did nothing to make that any easier for Apollonia.

"Oh. Sanctus," she said. "Sometimes when he has a bad day he will strike me. It isn't very often, and I understand . . ." her voice trailed off as Apollonia gave up trying to hide her distress.

"Onesimus' teacher taught him that husbands are supposed to love their wives just as Yeshua loved His followers. Yeshua *died* for His people, taking their punishment upon Himself," she explained. "I know it may be difficult now, but I know the God of Creation can *and will* help Sanctus to regain control so that he can be a Godly example in his home. I will discuss this with Onesimus tonight as we travel and we will pray together that Yeshua will give Sanctus a love that sacrifices self for his wife." Giving Marcella a light hug, she turned and began talking to the women about Yeshua and His sacrifice for them—not only for their husbands but for each and every woman who was there that day.

αω

CHAPTER NINETEEN

While traveling homeward, Onesimus didn't find it the least bit awkward to loop his arm around his darling's shoulders and control Poppy while embracing her whose head lay against his shoulder as murmured conversation drifted upward to his ears.

"I never thought sitting and talking could be as exhausting as a full day in the kitchens, but it certainly is!" Apollonia exclaimed. "Three of the women seem to think that as long as their husbands understand and believe, they have no need to believe for themselves and one came today with fresh bruises and a black eye!"

Her listener winced and tightened his hold on his wife. "Did she say how she—"

"Oh, yes. As if it were the most natural thing in the world! 'Sanctus had a bad day and sometimes he strikes me, but I understand . . . !' she said." Apollonia sat up straight, indignant for her student. "How can any woman believe that . . . ?"

"Now, Sweetheart," Onesimus broke in. "Not all women had the advantage of being a slave in a household of faith as you did" He stopped with a puzzled frown on his face. "...the advantage of being a slave. . ." he snorted and began to chuckle. The chuckle became a chortle and the chortle grew to a hearty belly laugh.

Apollonia turned sideways in the seat, watching in bewilderment as his laughter grew louder and more insistent until she replayed his words in her head. When she realized what he had said she began to giggle and the giggle grew to a gurgle and the gurgle to an outright, totally unlady-like burst of laughter.

With the two of them almost helpless with laughter, poor Poppy just stopped in the middle of the road and waited for further instruction from one of the silly people sitting behind her, guffawing insanely in the little pony cart she had been obediently pulling until the man directing her went crazy and she came to an unfamiliar crossroad. Then she thought it best to stop and wait for sanity to return.

Λ Ω

Onesimus guided the pony cart to its place behind Rhais' cottage. He unhitched Poppy and led her across the meadow to the barn where he watered her and gave her a goodly ration of hay and oats for her fine service. While she ate, he talked to her and took a curry comb and brushed her down. Then he patted her rump, gave her a fallen apple for a treat and secured her for the night.

As he approached the cottage, he could smell that dinner was ready on the hearth and he was more than ready for it! *How clever Apollonia is!* He marveled to himself. *Barley bread made this morning and set by the hearth to keep warm, some delicious cheese melted over the coals of the fire to dip the bread in, and some fresh vegetables from the kitchen garden and we have a wonderful supper.*

Washing his hands, he realized that there wasn't anything required before they could eat, so he sat at the table and smiled at his wife. Together they bowed their heads and prayed, "Lord God Jehovah how grateful we are for your provision and for this day. Bless this food to our bodies and bless all the meetings this Lord's Day to be food for our souls. In the name of Christ our Savior, Amen."

After the clearing up was done, the exhausted pair went to bed and, cuddling toward sleep, Onesimus murmured, "How blessed I have been to have been a slave!" he chuckled in remembrance of his earlier statement. "How blessed to have met and married this beautiful bride of mine who loves you, Lord, as much or more than I do! Thank you. Father . . ." and before he could get his "Amen" out, he was breathing deeply and evenly . . . and so was Apollonia.

αω

CHAPTER TWENTY

O nesimus stood in the cottage doorway and watched the slowly
falling snow. It seemed as if the clouds above were breaking
up and drifting lightly to the ground. He tossed an extra
cloak over his shoulders and set out for Philemon's home.

As he walked, he rehearsed what he had to say to make it sound
more palatable to his employer. As he reached the doorstep, he gave a
shout, "Ho the house! Is Philemon there?"

Philemon appeared at the door and smiled widely, "Useful One!
How wonderful to see you! What brings you out into the snow? Come
in and warm yourself as we talk."

Onesimus grasped Philemon's arm near the elbow and Philemon did
the same as they walked together into the sparklingly white home and
seated themselves on couches placed at right angles to a fireplace that
was busily warming the room.

"I'm interested to know how your tutoring of the Laodicean church
is going," Philemon said. "You've been going every Seventh Day since
just after harvest and here it is, inching toward leafing season again!
Why, this is probably the only snow we will see this year! By this time
next month we will be seeing hints of budding on the trees, I'm sure!"

Onesimus nodded along with everything Philemon said but he
hadn't really heard much because he was too busy planning his argument. Suddenly realizing that Philemon had fallen silent he opened his
mouth to speak but Philemon beat him to it. "You don't seem to be truly
listening, my friend. Is your heart so far away? How can I help you?"

The former slave closed his eyes and shook his head. "I'm sorry for
my inattentiveness. First, let me say that the Laodicean body is coming

along nicely and even our angry one has learned to put his anger aside rather than putting it on his long-suffering wife! But I come here because I have a great favor to ask you if I may."

Philemon smiled and sat back, leaning his elbow on the headrest of the couch with his right fist propping up his head. "Of course! And if it is possible, I will be glad to assist you."

Taking a deep breath, Onesimus began, "As you know, we have recently gotten word that our dear brother Paulus has received his martyr's crown by the swordsman's craft. While neither of us can do anything to help the Church of Rome right now, there are things we can do near here to carry on Paulus' work."

He paused for a breath and Philemon broke in, "I think I know where you are going with this, but please continue."

"Well, Paulus began new works all over this region including Laodicea where I help catechize every week. There are also new churches started either by Paulus or by others in Sardis, Smyrna, Lystra, Iconium, and other towns. I understand that most of these churches have been well-taught by those who started the work, but I also know that Lystra was dependent upon Paulus and Timothy and that Timothy has become too occupied with helping the bodies near Rome that Paulus founded to travel much. I am sure that there are other new churches facing the same kind of loss of leadership and I believe God is calling me to help these churches...I know that when the new growing season comes you will need me here but . . ."

Philemon allowed a small smile to cross his face as he held up his hand and, shaking his head, interrupted his former slave's anxious explanations. "Yes. I know what you're saying, and you are right."

Onesimus held his breath. He was afraid Philemon meant that he couldn't spare him.

"But did I not tell you last summer that I believed in the future you were going to do more for the body of Christ and less for the olive groves of Philemon? These churches do need teachers and with Quintin doing such a good job of helping you, I believe we could spare you for a couple more churches . . . say on Third Day and Fifth Day . . . and, since I don't have to pay a full salary to Quintin I will pay you the difference between your regular day's pay and what Quintin receives. However, I'm afraid I can't spare Apollonia that often. Will that hinder your work?"

Onesimus shook his head. "No. I didn't think you could lose your best cook every week and I've learned enough from her to teach both the men and women together. If you are certain that this will not cause you hardship I will write to Timothy and find out the names of the elders for the church at Lystra and one other that could use my help. I will keep you informed about what I learn."

While they talked, the sun had come out from behind the clouds, the clouds had stopped "breaking up", and the snow had melted and was watering the earth just as God had intended. So Onesimus took off the second cloak and, folding it over his arm, he trotted back to his cottage where he lunched on cold chicken and rye bread from last night's dinner. Next, he settled at the table with quill and ink to inscribe a missive for Timothy offering his help with the nearby churches in need.

αω

CHAPTER TWENTY-ONE

O nesimus leaned forward on his chair, his glance moving from one man to the next until all five of them had had the benefit of his gaze.

"So, if none of you feel ready to shepherd this group and you have no shepherd available, how do you hold your meetings?" He could hardly believe what he had been hearing. These men were good-hearted and truly believed the message they had heard—but they had no idea how to shepherd a growing group of believers.

Felician, who seemed to be the spokesman for the group, replied. "We meet here at my home and sometimes we have a traveler like Paulus or Timothy. When that is not the case, we just read from one of the three letters we have from Paulus or the Gospel of Mark or we talk about what has happened in our lives and how the great God, Yeshua, has been guiding us." His thick, black curls bounced on his head even more than Quintin's had as a boy, Onesimus thought with amusement.

"But that doesn't mean we make up the rules as we go!" Ulfilas, with the round baker's tummy broke in. "If we have need of special guidance, we pray for it and wait until an answer comes. We work hard to make certain that everything we do reflects the will of Yeshua and his Father."

"I am positive that is the case," Onesimus said with a smile. "However, Timothy and I agree that you really need help to learn and to grow. That is why I am here. I spent two years living and studying with Paulus and he taught me everything I needed to be faithful. I am here to pass that knowledge on to you."

Emilianus (a man whose slender form and graceful movements belied his ability to grab a sheep, shear it in three or four passes, and send it on its way) wept openly, "Brother Onesimus! We cannot pay you . . . this is a very poor body. To be sure there are two families who . . ."

"I am not here to earn money. I do this just as Paulus did it for me . . . freely, out of love for Yeshua and for my fellow believers," Onesimus broke in gently. "I will be here every week on Third Day to help you with things you may not know or understand. I also will try to copy some of the letters that my wealthy employer has managed to collect. Some of these were circulated from church to church and he copied them and a few he purchased for the people meeting at his home. This way, you will have more guidance from the Apostles' letters."

"We will feed you when you come. We can at least do that much!" Sabinus spoke for the first time. Short and skinny, Sabinus looked as if he hadn't had a good meal in months, but Onesimus had seen him eat at mid-day and knew he ate more than Ulfilas ever dreamed of consuming.

"That I will accept!" Onesimus said with a smile. "Now brothers, I must be starting for home, but I will see you and any who would like join us on Third Day next. Be advised that your mothers, wives, and daughters are to come, as well, for the basics of believing are important to all—male and female."

Anteros, the fifth elder of the body of Christ at Lystra, stood and draped his arm around Onesimus' shoulders. "We have been praying for some time that Yeshua would bring us a teacher and now, here you are!" His startlingly green eyes glistened with unshed tears and his red beard bristled as he spoke. It was obvious his hair had been red as well . . . it still was in the halo that surrounded the bare crown of his head. "Our women have also wanted help and they will be so pleased to know you are coming! We thank God for you, Brother, and can barely wait until Third Day!"

After a session of prayer together, Onesimus mounted the pony cart and turned Poppy toward home.

Λ Ω

"I am surprised they have been able to do as much as they have with no teacher to help them and only occasional visits from Paulus and Timothy," Onesimus told Philemon after taking care of Poppy. "The great God of Israel has certainly done great things to keep them safe!"

"Of course! Look what He did to get *you*!" Philemon replied with a chuckle. "Drive you all the way to Rome so that you could find the truth that was offered to you right here!"

Onesimus raised his eyebrows and rolled his eyes. "That was amazing, wasn't it?"

"Amazing for you . . . inconvenient for me!"

Onesimus laughed and shrugged, "We must not complain about God's methods . . .," he stated with a false pretention.

Philemon gave his shoulder a light jab. "Complain!" he said. "I'll show you complain, you pompous jackanapes!"

"Seriously, we need to help these people all we can," Onesimus said. "From what they have told me, they have a whole storehouse full of nothing. There are only a couple of families who have managed to stay afloat recently. The others work at jobs that used to make decent money but because they refuse to burn incense to Caesar, their neighbors are afraid the authorities may think they are Christians if they give support to these believers so they are having trouble earning enough to keep food on their tables."

Philemon crossed his arms and frowned, staring at the ground. "So far, you are teaching at Laodicea on Seventh Day and you begin teaching at Lystra this coming Third Day," he muttered quietly. "On Fifth Day you will be going to whatever body Timothy deems in most need of a teacher as soon as you hear from him. . ." he looked up at Onesimus. "Tomorrow, I think I will travel to our fellow believers in the area and see if we can raise some donations for you to take with you this next Third Day. Will that help?"

Onesimus couldn't hide the huge smile that split his face in half. "Thank you! I know that will help a great deal!" He shook Philemon's hand vigorously and headed for the little cottage that held the only person in the world that truly knew what a tender and loving man he was.

αω

CHAPTER TWENTY TWO

Apollonia and Onesimus stood in amazement watching as their brothers and sisters in Christ assembled for the meeting that Lord's Day.

As every other Lord's Day, there were baskets of fish and baskets of breads. There were platters of meats and sacks of fruit and all of it was laid out on the groaning tables brought from the kitchens. But this Lord's Day, Andrew the tentmaker was missing from the walkers who came bearing breakfast and the mid-day meal. At first concern creased Onesimus' face, but Philemon patted his arm and said, "Do not fret yourself. Andrew will be here shortly."

The believers and non-believers relieved the tables of their burdens and stood or sat visiting and catching up on the latest news as they ate until Philemon called for the believers to gather round the table for the Lord's Supper. As they walked toward the tables, Onesimus was stunned to see Andrew pulling into the yard in a small wagon owned by Philemon and drawn by Poppy. Questions flew through his mind . . . why was Andrew using Philemon's small wagon? Why was he using Poppy? What was all that stuff in the bed of the wagon?

Andrew jumped down from the wagon's seat and led Poppy to a shady area. "Onesimus," he called as he approached the gathering. "The Body of Christ at Colossae would like you to take these gifts and distribute them to the believers at Lystra. I apologize for being a little late, but I collected more than I anticipated, so it took a little longer."

Smilingly, Philemon said, "It's no trouble! Break your fast and we will celebrate the Lord's Supper after you have eaten." Turning toward Onesimus he asked with a grin, "Will you be able to handle this task?"

Onesimus was still so amazed he found it hard to reply but reply, he did. "I am so grateful to all those who gave so generously and to those who had nothing to give but gave their prayers! Thank you all so much!"

It wasn't long before those who had come were seated in the house, on the porch, in the yard, wherever they could find room and were quieting their minds and listening with their hearts to what the Spirit would say to the Church.

A young boy of about eight began to sing, "O God of Peace! Restoring hope to all who hear thy voice," rang out over the people as they began to pick up the harmonious humming to accompany his clear and sweet tenor. "How lovely are your splendors; how gracious is your mercy! In joy we come to worship you, surrender to your loving ways, and bow before your throne in awe and wonder!"

Suddenly, Onesimus' jaw dropped as he recognized this child. This eight-year-old with the sweet spirit and lovely voice was Felix! The child who was run down by a Centurion's horse and brought by his parents to the very first meeting Onesimus had ever attended. The child who lay in his father's arms as the parents ran into the house and begged for prayer for their poor, dead son…the son who promptly sat up and demanded, "Want down! Want down NOW!" The boy who was now raising his silver voice in adoration to Yahweh!

Tears flowed freely down the cheeks of Onesimus as he reached for Apollonia's hand. "Do you know who . . . ?"

"Of course, Dear! I thought you knew him all along!" she whispered back.

Looking into her beautiful gray eyes, he shook his head in wonder. "It was only as I heard him singing that I realized who he was."

The service continued with some telling of petty persecutions God had brought them through, some giving witness to the power of God, some requesting prayer for needs they had, and woven through all of it, the peace and joy that works in all believers' hearts was evident.

Λ Ω

On Third Day Onesimus went to Philemon and asked if he should use a larger horse . . . perhaps the bay gelding that hadn't been exercised in a week or so. There was a large cargo that needed to be taken to Lystra and he was afraid Poppy, the little mare he usually used, was going to suffer if she had to travel so far with such a load.

Philemon doubted that it would hurt Poppy, she was after all, a work horse. But he was willing to allow Onesimus to take the gelding instead since it *was* quite a weight for such a small horse. Besides, he said, the bay really did need some exercise so shortly after sunrise Onesimus harnessed the bay and backed him into the traces of the still-filled wagon.

Before starting on his journey to Lystra Onesimus also made sure that his short dagger-like sword was carefully stored under his seat. He had a rich cargo and was determined that it would make it to the dear people it was collected for.

He hadn't traveled two full leagues from the house before he thought he would have to put that sword to use. He was jouncing along, singing joy-filled songs to God and paying small attention to the road when that inner voice spoke clearly, *Pay attention, Child! Around that next curve are two robbers who await a full wagon to attack."*

Onesimus had learned to listen to the voice, because it was the voice of the Holy Spirit communicating truth to believers when needed so he stopped singing and started praying. First in his own language and then in the special prayer language the Holy Spirit used so that the enemy of our souls couldn't understand what was being said. As he rounded the curve, he slapped the reins on the horse's hind quarters and the gelding picked up speed, cantering beside a large rock outcropping where Onesimus knew the robbers hid.

At first, Onesimus' idea was just to speed by and keep going but, instead, he pulled the wagon to a full stop. Then he called out to the invisible robbers, "Ho the rock! I want to let you know that the God of the Jews . . . my God as well . . . wants you to know he loves you. His only son came to earth to die for you so that you could be clean of all your sin! It is for your sake I was sent this way so that you could hear this good news!"

Silence followed the short echoes of his voice. Then there came a rattle and clatter from behind the rock and the bushes began to shake violently as two men came around the rock and stood in the road. Onesimus took one look at the two men and began to shake his head. "I cannot believe that you have chosen me again!"

The dark-haired, heavily muscled man glanced at his partner with a puzzled look. His partner just gazed back and shrugged.

"You attacked my wife and me on the road out of Colossae a while back. You wanted to take her with you. Do you remember now?"

Both men's jaws dropped as Onesimus reached once again under his seat and pulled out his short sword. "Ah! I see you *do* remember now."

Without another word, the erstwhile robbers backed away, while beginning to bow and salute, mumbling, "So sorry, gov'nor! Some mistake here! We're only wishing to bid you good day, sir!"

"Stop!" Onesimus shouted. "I have good news for you. Would you like to hear it?"

Both men stopped and glanced at each other. Then, obviously feeling threatened by the short sword flashing before them, they nodded.

"Well and well!" Onesimus replied. "Why don't you have a seat on that convenient rock right there and I will tell you the story of how much Yahweh loves you and what he is willing to do for you!" and he proceeded to give them the Gospel, which they embraced with joy. Onesimus invited them to accompany him as he brought the much-needed supplies to the believers in Lystra. "Besides," Onesimus explained. "I could use your help unloading and distributing these things to the Church there."

Probus and Sixtus (for such were their names) were more than happy to accompany Onesimus to Lystra and to help with the supplies as a way to show gratitude for the mercy they had found at the feet of the Savior.

Λ Ω

The wagon rumbled into the street where Felician resided. While the property sat directly on the street, the house had a wall that connected to its right side and stretched about 10 cubits (or 15 feet) to the street corner. The wall turned the corner and traveled for another 20 cubits and then turned another corner to return again to the house, where it was attached to the rear wall on the right side. The front wall had a gate-opening about four cubits from the house wall and this is where Onesimus turned into the garden. Felician along with Sabinus and Felician's wife, Maura, hurried out the house's kitchen door when they heard the wagon creaking along into their courtyard but stopped in shock, staring at what they were seeing. There was their Catechist, driving a huge horse with a coat that, in a human, would be called auburn. Beside him on the seat sat a small, thin fellow resembling nothing so much as a weasel and, in the body of the wagon atop a load of "stuff" sat a big burly man with bad teeth seen through the huge smile on his face.

Onesimus jumped down from the seat and, giving a handclasp to both men and a slight bow toward Maura, he introduced his two riders.

"My brothers and sister! I would like you to meet Sixtus the fellow on the seat, and Probus. They have just heard the Good News and have decided to join us. They came along today to help unload the wagon and to meet their new family."

Probus and Sixtus made their way to stand beside Onesimus and spoke to the three. "To be open with you, we were going to rob our friend of all these worldly goods . . . but he turned the tables on us and told us the Grand Story. We were raised by good people and can do all sorts of carpentry work . . . but for years we found it easier to simply take from others what we wanted. Now, we will begin doing honorable work and, with your help, we will learn truth and walk in The Way!"

Maura was the first to respond. "Yeshua takes all who come to him so who are we to judge?" Turning toward Onesimus she asked, "What is all this?"

"*This,*" Onesimus replied with a grin, "is a wagon full of brotherly love from fellow believers in Colossae. When they were told of the believers' plight here in Lystra, they began piling things they felt you could use into the wagon. Those things Lystra's believers can use will stay here but if there are things that aren't needed here, they will be sent on to another church with needs or it will be sold in the marketplace here and the money raised can be used for whatever is needed."

Felician and Sabinus had already moved to the wagon and had begun unloading it, placing the items on the sides of the walkways of the courtyard. "Maura," Felician said, "call Domitius and send him to the houses of the other believers. Tell him to let them know there is a bounty of necessities in our courtyard for them to come select from."

Maura smiled and nodded and moved toward the house to rouse their fourteen-year-old son from his customary afternoon slumbers.

Probus, Sixtus, and Onesimus joined the two elders in their task. It took no time at all and the wagon was unloaded, the bay was led off for water and some nice, green grass, and the men were seated in the shace of beech and chestnut trees in the courtyard as Onesimus prepared to work with these precious souls to teach them more of The Way than they had known before.

αω

CHAPTER TWENTY THREE

Philemon pulled the branch of the olive tree carefully toward himself. He smiled and glanced over at Onesimus and Apollonia who were walking with him.

"Looks like another good crop, my friends!" he observed. "See here?" He grabbed Onesimus by the arm and pulled him toward the branch.

"See how the blossoms, though tiny, all have four healthy white petals and a center of brilliant yellow? You see those green anthers surrounding the center? When the blossom has both parts, anther and pistil, it can make olives all by itself! That's the way my trees are. God breathes the wind through the blossoms and they become olives. What a miracle olives are! And the blossoms smell sweet, as well. Don't you agree Apollonia?"

Every May, when the blossoms burst forth on the olive trees, Onesimus had learned that Philemon would wax poetic. Onesimus smothered a grin as he was pulled along in Philemon's right hand. He glanced at his wife being tugged along in Philemon's left hand and she quickly looked away before she burst out laughing. There was no doubt that Philemon loved his work and believed that no one could be exposed to the mysteries of the olive tree for very long without being as completely overwhelmed with amazement as he was at God's wonderful machinery he had built into the twisted, gnarled branches of the gray-green trees.

The weekly stroll Philemon took through the olive groves surrounding his home was something he looked forward to all through the chilly winter months. On days that were bearable, he often wrapped his special thickly woven cloak around himself and wandered out to look over his beloved trees. He would step inside his olive press and breathe in the olive-scented air. Sometimes he would even pass his hands over the presses and, at all times, he prayed for his family, his olives, his presses, his workers, and his slaves. He would get lost in prayer as he stood within the walls of his press and would beg God's guidance in how to relate to his workers and his slaves and how to treat his slaves in such a way as to draw as many as possible into an honest relationship with Yeshua so that he could break the chains of slavery both of body and soul.

Onesimus loved Philemon as a brother in Christ and was extremely indebted to his late, beloved Paulus and to Philemon for freeing him from both the angry bitterness and unforgiveness he had harbored toward his father and for releasing him from his earthly bondage and making him a freeman again. Even so, he knew there was soon to come a time when there would be a great change both in his and Apollonia's life and in the life of Philemon, as well.

Oh, yes. It would come . . . and it wasn't that far away . . . but for now he would bide his time and hold his silence, until the Lord Yeshua, told him to speak.

Apollonia knew as well that change was coming. Change such as she had never known. Having been a slave from the age of 14 until Philemon freed her because of his reluctance to hold a Christian sister or brother in chains, in the flesh, Apollonia wasn't certain that such changes as God had whispered to her and as Onesimus had revealed to her were going to be changes for the better. But she was willing to change wherever the Lord moved them to do so.

Λ Ω

Apollonia sat watching Onesimus as he scrubbed the top of his head with his left hand and chomped down on the oaten cake and roasted egg she had prepared for his breakfast. She rose from the table and grabbed the comb from the cabinet and, approaching on tiptoe as if to keep from startling a wild animal, she combed through the shiny black curls on her beloved's head.

"Here! What are you doing, woman?" he cried out with a laugh. "You know you cannot EVER tame that wild hair of mine!"

"I know, husband . . . but I must try. Especially since you insist on scrubbing your pate with that big paw of yours, making the tangles worse than the way they grow!" she replied with good humor.

"Aren't you going to break your fast before heading to the kitchens?"

"No. I think I will just have an apple for now. Besides," and she tossed her head saucily, "I am head cook! I'll eat whatever I want!" she exclaimed as she headed toward the door.

Chuffing softly, Onesimus raised his right arm (complete with oaten cake still held in his fingers) and waved at her as if to pooh-pooh her words. "Of course you will! That's why all the workers and slaves are starving! You eat it all before it reaches the table!"

Crossing back to the table, she playfully beat him about the head and shoulders. "How dare you! Are you saying I'm a glutton? I think I am owed an apology!"

Onesimus just ducked his head and laughed before grabbing her around the waist and pulled her to him. Since he was seated and she, standing, he turned his face and laid it against her tummy. "Just see what a wonderful woman you have given me Lord!" he shouted. "I love her with everything that is not dedicated to loving You!"

After a final hug, Apollonia left for the kitchens and Onesimus readied himself for the early summer tasks of reconciling the books from the winter's expenses and preparing the inks and quills he would need for the summer's work ahead.

αω

CHAPTER TWENTY FOUR

O nesimus stood in the shade of the cypress tree contemplating the tip-tilted pony cart he used for his weekly trips into Lystra and Laodicea. His fisted hands on his hips, his elbows jutting sharply out to the sides, he was the very picture of irritated man-hood.

"If it's not one thing it's another!" he muttered to himself. "How am I supposed to put this wheel back on by myself? Harvest is on and everyone who isn't needed in the olive press is busy beating the trees and gathering olives! Tomorrow I've got to be in Lystra and, for that, I *could* just ride Poppy . . . but on Seventh Day, when Apollonia comes with me, I *must* have this cart!" he grimaced and kicked gently at the wheel that was still where it belonged . . . but not too hard! It might come off as well!

Sighing mightily, he paced around the cart, considering all the ways he might be able to lift the cart so he could affix the cart wheel back in place. Finally, he came up with a plan. Hurrying to the stables, he found a length of rope, a large hammer, and a long spike, used to nail thick beams into place. Then, back to the cart where he took the spike and drove it three or four inches deep into the back corner of the cart, leaving half of it exposed. Next, he tied a slipknot in one end of the rope and hooked it over the nail-head. He tossed the rope over the lowest limb of the tree (it only took three tries!) and returned to the stables where he slipped a collar and reins onto the big bay. Then, leading the bay to the pony cart, he fastened the end of the rope dangling from the tree-limb to the collar and began leading the horse away from the cart.

As he had hoped, the cart rose slowly into the air and, the big bay being what he was . . . big . . . never even felt the drag of the rope and cart on his shoulders. He tied off the reins and hurried to the cart where he lifted the wheel back onto the axel and drove a couple of pins through the wheel and into the axel. When he thought he was done, he seized both sides of the wheel and threw himself backwards, trying his best to pull the wheel off again. When the wheel remained on the axel without moving and rattling, he knew his job was good and he could trust the wheel to carry his most precious cargo . . . his wife . . . to Laodicea. The trip to Lystra by himself in the morning would be a final test of his cartwrighting skills!

Slowly backing the horse to lower the cart back to earth, Onesimus talked reassuringly to him and patted his nose several times. When the cart was firmly on the ground, Onesimus freed the horse of the rope and took him and the rope back to the stables. He then returned and removed the spike from the back of the cart and took it and the hammer back as well. Then he went to find Philemon and report what he had done.

Λ Ω

"Ho the house!" came the shout. Apollonia and Onesimus looked at one another and shrugged. "Ho the house!" the shout came again and they both stood from the table where they had been eating and moved toward the door. Once again, the shout came, "Ho! The house!" before they could reach the door.

As the third shout died away, Onesimus opened the door and stood staring at their visitor.

"I thought I would come see you and bring you the latest news," Protos laughed as he jumped from his horse to the ground. "Little brother there are such things as I must tell you!" This last was said as he was wrapped in a warm embrace from his brother.

"Well, let's sit here on the porch where there is a little breeze," Onesimus suggested and they sat while Apollonia brought each of them a glass of honey mead and a generous piece of honey cake.

These duties done, Apollonia was going to return to the house as a good wife did when her husband was entertaining a guest, but Protos spoke quickly, "No! Do not leave us fair Apollonia! What I say here is as important for you to hear as your husband." And so, she sat down beside Onesimus and listened quietly as Protos began.

"Father has not been well these last five-month. He may go for weeks and seem hale and hearty, but suddenly he will begin to shake and shiver with ague. He says he feels as if his head is floating in a water bath. Sometimes he speaks nonsense and sometimes he doesn't speak at all. He talks about our faces melting and all the time he is shaking and wrapping himself in blankets to get warm, he is burning up with fever. Then, just as suddenly as the fever and delirium come on him, the fever breaks and within an hour or so he is back to his own self."

Protos stopped to take a long draught and shook his head. "It is very possible that a miasma from our land is causing it as Hippocrates suggested and sometimes we are almost convinced that someone has cursed him but since our household has claimed the Name we know that that is *not* the answer. It's just very hard to understand. You know Father has opened our house for weekly meetings, do you not? We have a very able teacher who was taught by Apollos, but with father being ill there have been times when we wondered if we would be able to host the meeting.

"That worry has now passed from us because another family—in fact, the family that purchased our old house—has offered to take the meetings into their home! They became believers shortly after your visit to us, when Father thought it would be a good thing to befriend them. It was only a matter of perhaps two full moons before he had won them to Yeshua . . . the man is pure power when it comes to evangelizing!"

Onesimus leaned forward and looked deeply into Protos' eyes. "Why are you here, my brother? There is more to this visit than simply a health report on our father, I am sure."

Protos drew in a deep breath and nodded. "Yes. There is." He looked away from Onesimus and back again. "There have been terrible rumblings lately of persecutions of Christians not only in Rome but as far away as southern Anatolia. I came here mostly to let you know that we are not safe just because we aren't Roman. Be careful, little brother, who you talk to and what you say!"

"I must speak to whomever Yeshua directs me to, Protos! You should understand that."

"Oh, I do. I certainly do! But be sure it is Yeshua who directs you. A dear friend of ours—one who came regularly to our meetings and loved Yeshua with all his being—was taken last Fourth Day! No one has seen him since and his poor wife is so worried she can neither eat nor sleep for fear. I believe it might be better for her if she could just know that the man is at home with Christ rather than wondering where he is, if he is being tortured or what has happened to him. The only thing she knows for certain is that he was on his way to visit a man who had left our fellowship about a fortnight before."

Onesimus bowed his head and shook it slowly. "This is sad news… *bad* news. I will be as careful as God will allow, I promise. I would also take this time to ask you to look after Apollonia if I am taken . . ."

At her name Apollonia, who had been considering what she would need to create the perfect Shepherd's Pie for Philemon's household as well as for her home, pricked up her ears and began to listen closely to what was being said.

" . . . I know that Philemon will deal fairly with her, but I would like to know that she will be cared for by my family in that case."

"Husband! Do not talk like that, I beg you!" she exclaimed with shock.

Onesimus shook his head and looked into her eyes. "You heard what Protos has said, haven't you?"

At her nod, he continued, "Then you must realize that the only sensible thing to do is to make arrangements for our loved ones in case the worse happens. If I am taken, I want you to have control of your destiny . . . but I also want to know that you aren't left with no choices at all. Especially if we leave this place sometime in the future, I need to know that you will be provided for and protected by my family and especially my brother. Is that acceptable with you, my dear?"

Looking at the porch floor, her lips a tightened line and her eyes in a squint, she slowly nodded her agreement. "Yes. I understand and I am thankful that I have a mate who will care for me even if it's from the g— the gr—the grave."

"Brother . . . Apollonia . . ." Protos' voice was solemnity itself. "You know that I will do everything in my power to make sure that Apollonia is provided for if necessary. Just don't do anything to help make it my duty if you can help it."

αω

CHAPTER TWENTY-FIVE

*T*imothy of Agapetus, to my dear brother Onesimus. Grace
and peace to you in your daily labors for our Christ,
 It is with great joy and deep sorrow that I pen these words
to you for there is much to be joyful about and also much to be
disquieted about. First, I find much joy in the growth of our
numbers within the city of Rome and in the wider fields of
harvest! Our numbers increase so rapidly that, from one Lord's
Day to the next there are new people who have come to The Way
through the leading of those who love and serve the Savior. It is a
rare week, indeed, when I am not called upon to meet with a new
believer and a rare New Moon when we do not begin a class to
catechize those who have come to The Faith.
 I understand, as well, that you have your hands full catechiz-
ing Lystra and Laodicea and are now asking for a third class to
work with. After much prayer and consideration, though, I think
you need to remain at your present posts until your students
are ready to be received into full fellowship. I know that your
employer(and former master), Philemon, is willing to give place
to your calling, but, for now, let us leave things as they stand.
Perhaps, after the harvest is complete, there may be time to either
add a third class to your circuit or to explore some other calling
you may be considering.
 Now, for the sorrow that I feel, I hesitate to share details
with you fearing that you may decide to make a stand against the
authorities who have brought this persecution upon your brothers

and sisters in Colossae, Corinth, and Ephesus and I beg of you, do it not! Nevertheless, this is something you need to be aware of.

As you have no doubt heard by now, Caesar Nero issued an edict declaring the persecution of those who follow The Way after the destroying fire that devastated this great city. Many of our number have been thrown to the lions, beheaded, as our dear Paulus, and even used as human torches hanging by chains and burning to light the darkened streets of Rome. At times, the whole city smells of the burning bodies of Christians. I find it painful but altogether fitting that believers should light the darkness of the Roman night as I am sure you do as well.

These persecutions continue to this day, but what I am now hearing is that the persecutions are reaching far beyond Rome to Greece and Macedonia as well as Anatolia, Syria, and even Jerusalem itself! I am grief-stricken that my own dear twin, Thomas, was taken last Seventh Day and is now at home with the Father.

The reason I am writing this to you though, is to urge you, my beloved brother in Yeshua, to remain faithful to Christ whatever is required of you. The teaching you have been doing must continue until the foundation is firmly established. When you believe that to be the case, with much prayer, appoint a shepherd to oversee the work so that you may become more flexible in your calling because in days of persecution many of us must be able to step into different roles at different times and you are one who has the training and the knowledge to do that.

I rejoice with you in your freedom and your marriage!

It is important for you to know the sign that our persecuted brothers and sisters use to identify each other. It is Iesous Xristos Theou Yios Sotare (Jesus Christ, Son of God, Savior) . . . Ichthus or fish. The first draws one half and the other completes the picture. Remember the sign for it may mean your life in the near future!

My prayers and the prayers of all the Roman brethren are with you and your household.

May the God and Father of our Lord, Jesus Christ be with you and keep you in His ways, Timothy.

Onesimus lowered the missive to his lap, unaware of the troubled frown that played around his mouth and on his forehead. He unrolled the very end of the letter and studied the secret sign again.

So *that* was what the traveler was doing when he drew that strange curve in the dirt! The man's horse was enjoying a rest inside the cool barn with some hay and water while the man himself sat quietly on his porch step resting before continuing his journey.

Onesimus stood up from his seat beside the man and walked deliberately to the simple arc the stranger had drawn in the yard. Picking up a stick, Onesimus drew another arc underneath the first one, creating a picture of a fish. Then, he looked up at the man and, smiling, tossed the stick to the side and stepped forward to grasp the man by both upper arms and embrace him. The man smiled back as tears sprang to his eyes.

"My name is Basil," he explained. "I am a friend of Timothy and when he found out that I was traveling into the Greek countryside he asked me if I would be near Colossae. When I confirmed that Colossae was on my route, he held me in his salon as he wrote this letter for you. I am afraid I am not going back to Rome for some time because my mother has called me home to Anatolia because she is very ill."

Onesimus shook his head, "There is no need for a reply, Basil. I am saddened to hear of the persecutions in Rome but already knew that some Christians in Colossae have been taken. I am especially sorry to hear that Thomas is gone, but I understand that his blood will water the ground and raise up new believers!

"I thank you for bringing this to me and pray protection for you traveling in these dangerous times."

At Basil's consent, Onesimus laid his hands on Basil's head and prayed, "Lord Yeshua, I ask for Basil's protection from brigands and the evils one may encounter on the roads. Keep him in your hands of mercy and take him safely to his mother's home. In the name of the God of Israel, Amen."

After Basil brought his mount into the yard and took his leave, Philemon came hurrying across the yard.

"Onesimus my friend! Have you the time to come to the press? I am in dire need of someone who can help in the pressing while Quintin reconciles his figures for the month," he queried. Then, seeing the fish drawn in the dirt, he glanced at the rider who was just leaving the yard and looked steadily at Onesimus. "Is there something I should understand as to why you have drawn a fish in the dirt?"

Onesimus forced a smile through his sorrow and replied, "It seems that with the persecutions, Christians have found a way to identify each other. One draws one half of the fish and the other person draws the other half." Then the two turned and started for the press as Onesimus completed his explanation.

αω

Chapter Twenty-Six

Apollonia went toward the olive press hoping to catch Onesimus before he left the building for the short walk across the olive grove to their cottage. She had come to revel in the walk with her beloved because it was a time when the cares of her work lay behind her both in a figurative and a literal sense and the cares of her household lay before her in the same way but neither was in the now. For these few minutes she and her husband could simply "be", talking about whatever came to mind . . . or talking about nothing and simply walking hand-in-hand, signaling their love for one another through the simple warmth of physical contact.

She glanced toward the place where a new house, not as grand as the Master's home but fine in its own right, was rising from the sun-drenched meadow. It was nearly complete and by the end of harvest it would be ready to welcome the newest member to Philemon's family, Quintin's bride, Quinta. As she watched, Quinta came around the corner of the new house and, knowing not that she was observed, clapped her hands with delight and skipped lightly up to the unfinished doorway.

"Ho! Wife!" The call came from Onesimus as he stepped from the press and saw Apollonia crossing toward him. Raising her hand in greeting, she beamed a great smile and as they came together, she took his hand and laughed. "Quinta is visiting her future home and is charmed with how it's coming together!" she said.

"And just how do you know that, woman?" Onesimus said with a low growl of pretend disapproval.

"'Tis simple to see. Open your eyes, dear husband, and glance over there," she tossed her thumb over her shoulder toward the new construction. "Is she not still over there, clapping her approval and skipping like a girl half her age?"

Onesimus glanced over and nodded in amazement. "So she is! Do all women behave like that? . . . Do YOU my dearest dear?"

"I'm certain that not all women skip and clap with joy . . . I can't imagine your mother hopping around like that—but I do when my delight is complete. I do it a lot, sweet fig, when I think of something joyful I have to tell you."

And with that, she dropped Onesimus hand and went skipping carefully across the yard as if she were a girl of ten instead of a woman of twenty.

Onesimus ran after her and, grasping her about her waist as they entered their own yard he looked deeply into her eyes. "When you have something joyful to tell me?" He tilted his head and stared at her. "Is this display just a demonstration? Or do you have something joyful to tell me?"

She wrinkled her nose and murmured, "Later, dearest. It IS joyful news . . . but you will have to wait a little longer before I tell you."

"Now this is truly unfair!" he cried in protest. "If you have good news then it isn't fair that you keep it from me! I demand . . . " but he was cut off by a light cuff on his nose.

"Later, I said! Let me prepare our supper and then, when we sit down to sup, I will tell you all about it."

Grumbling lightly, Onesimus let her go and followed her into the house where the barley bread baked this morning lent its fragrance to the air.

Ten minutes later the two of them were seated at their table. Before them were fresh slices of the bread Apollonia had made, along with the last fragments of a piece of ham she had come home with the day before. Also on the table was a bowl with figs, another holding green onions and leeks, and another with almonds. After giving thanks to God for His provision, the two began to serve themselves and Onesimus said, "All right. We are seated at the table; we are partaking in this wonderful repast. Now, wife, keep your promise and tell me your good news."

Apollonia gave him a sideways glance and said quietly, "You must guess. Two guesses and if you don't guess true, THEN I will tell you."

"*Woman!*" He cried in exasperation, "*You promised!*"

"I promised I would tell you, but I didn't tell you the conditions. Now guess!" She said primly.

Rolling his eyes he said, "Oh, well, let's see . . . what could make my wife skip like a child? What . . . Hmmm . . . Apphia has given you some new clothing she no longer desires?"

"No! That isn't joyful news . . . that's *nice* news but not joyful news!" she giggled.

"Hummmmmmm . . . well, then . . ." he skewed his mouth to the side and squinted his eyes. "Philemon complimented your cooking and gave you a baby goat to raise as a reward."

This brought a guffaw from Apollonia. "Now what kind of joyful news would that be? Just more work for me!"

"Well," the rejoinder came. "I guessed twice now you must tell me . . . what is your joyful news?"

Instead of answering Apollonia stood up and turned sideways to Onesimus. She stood there and smoothed her hand down over her belly. "Do you notice anything?" She asked quietly.

"Aaaarrrrgh! Woman! I demand you tell me immediately . . ." he stopped and looked carefully at his beloved. "Are you growing fatter?" That would be good news because everyone knew that fat people were healthier than thin people.

She tilted her head to one side and then said, "Well, I have grown fatter, but not as fat as I will be . . ."

Onesimus poked his head forward a little and tilted it to the left. "Apple of my eye, PLEASE! I AM IN AGONY HERE! Are you telling me . . . ?"

Her smile and nod brought him to his feet. He grasped her around the waist and danced across the room to the music of their joyful laughter. Then he gasped and lowered her gently to her seat. "Are you fairing well? You are in good health? Oh! My!" he headed toward the door and then turned and ran back to her side. Taking her hands in his, he said, "Now, sit there until I return, I have to tell Philemon so that he will lighten your duties . . ." he dropped her hands and started again for the door.

"Onesimus!" she cried out in delight. "There is no need for that! Everything is fine. I am fine, as far as I can tell the baby is fine! We will go together in the morning to tell Philemon just because he should know NOT because he needs to lighten my load! I have Gozbert to do all my lifting and such."

With that voice of wisdom, Onesimus came back to his wife and, picking her up, carried her to the bed where he seated her on the straw-filled mattress. "Fine. Tomorrow morning, first thing. But you stay right there," he dropped Apollonia's sewing basket beside her, "and spend this evening doing something quiet. I will take care of cleaning up. My beloved," he crooned. "The mother of my child! For this night you will rest and I will do the chores."

αω

CHAPTER TWENTY-SEVEN

The harvest had come and gone and Quintin had handled all the bookkeeping for it without needing Onesimus' help even once. The books were balanced, the olives were pressed, the oil was stored in amphorae ready to be taken into Ephesus and shipped.

Apollonia was beginning to waddle a little when she walked but hadn't yet begun to feel the back strain that often comes in the last two or three months of pregnancy. Onesimus was still walking around with his chest puffed out almost as far as his wife's tummy and never tired of telling everyone who passed by on the road that his wife was going to have his baby.

It was a sunny, warm Seventh Day and Onesimus had concluded the Catechism class for Laodicea. Since Apollonia was beginning to be uncomfortable when she traveled, she had stopped coming with him and had turned her women over to Onesimus' teaching. He had done well with them and they were ready to become full-members of the body of Christ. That particular piece of business would be concluded with the local bishop in attendance. Both Onesimus and Apollonia would be there in the afternoon of the following day, (the Lord's Day) They would travel to Laodicea in style since Philemon had promised they could use the special carriage that had well-sprung seats and a shady roof.

As Onesimus looked back over his time with the Laodiceans he smiled with satisfaction. A pastor had been chosen from among them and would take up his duties on the morrow. Onesimus was satisfied that he had done a good work for God there and that soon another town would also have a church of local members . . . Lystra.

Apollonia was seated under the cypress tree when Onesimus came home. She waved at him and gestured him over. Taking his hand, she placed it gently on the side of her swelling belly.

Thump! Thump! Onesimus started and pulled his hand back. He stared at her and a grin began to grow across his face. He put his hand back on her tummy. *Thump! Thumthump!* "My son has a strong kick, doesn't he?"

"He does!" Apollonia smiled. "Or she!"

"Woman!" he growled. "You had better give me a boy!"

"*I* am not giving you *anything*!" She replied pertly. "The *Father* is. So, you need to threaten Him if you want to guarantee a boy!"

Onesimus nodded and wrapped his arms around her. "You are so right. He gave me you when I needed you most. And now He is giving me exactly what I need now. I will never threaten Him—a measure of bravery I have yet to master—and I will be overjoyed whatever our child is."

"This harvest's numbers are perfect, Quintin! You've got it down!" Onesimus crowed as he slapped the scroll down in front of the young man seated beside him. "You have just stolen my job from me!"

Quintin grinned his lopsided grin and shook his head. "Oh no, Onesimus! You can't get out of it that easily! I'm going to need you around to check my figures and make sure I haven't made some mistake that will make a couple of amphorae of olive oil to disappear!"

The two laughed together as they remembered the debacle that caused Onesimus to run away and find his soul's freedom in Rome.

Quintin's grandfather was more than a little moon-touched and had taken two amphorae of oil so he could oil himself up and slip out of the clutches of the angel of death. But he hadn't told Philemon or anyone what he was going to do so Onesimus had felt the finger of suspicion pointing at him. He was so afraid that he would be treated as his family had treated *their* dishonest slaves with beatings and even death . . . that Onesimus ran from Philemon's household and met Paulus. From him Onesimus learned more about Yeshua and his mercy and found freedom of heart and soul. After two years serving Paulus and learning about his own new life he returned to Philemon with a letter from Paulus urging Philemon to "accept Onesimus back as a brother".

Those remembered days of pain, bitterness, and trouble didn't bring tears or sadness to the former slave, though. It brought only joy that God had used a madman and Onesimus' own anger and fear to bring him into the Kingdom of God. It reminded him clearly of the day shortly after his conversion when Paulus had comforted a saddened Onesimus by saying, "It doesn't matter whether we count an event as a good thing or a bad thing . . . God uses both good and bad things to work out in our lives what he has planned for us. He turns even very bad events into good and all we must do is trust that he is working everything, bad and good, into something wonderful for our lives."

Onesimus patted his protégé on his shoulder and spoke again. "Quintin, I am certain you now can do as fine a job for your father as I have always tried to do. There will come a time not too far away when I will be busy doing other things and YOU will have the full charge of your father's books. I know you will do a wonderful job." Then, placing his finger to his lips in the universal sign for silence, Onesimus smiled and walked away.

CHAPTER TWENTY-EIGHT

The early weeks of summer came and went with sun and rain, blue skies and gray. The trees' blossoms began to bud and create small "berries" that would grow and become first, green olives that were slightly bitter to the taste which would ripen into the beautiful black olives that became fruit for the table and oil for the markets.

Apollonia was busy teaching the cooks who were under her in the kitchen how to maintain the standard of meals that she had set when she had first become head cook. While the cooks were curious, her lessons were so subtle that they were never sure they were being taught anything, let alone learning how to take the place of Philemon's head cook when the changes Onesimus and Apollonia anticipated became reality. Even if they *did* recognize her lessons for what they were, no doubt they summed it all up as making things ready so she could be gone for several weeks, recovering from the birth of the child she expected in late Fifth-month, or July, or early Sixth-month at the latest.

Both Laodicea and Lystra had done well in the catechisms and now had full-fledged congregations full of members who knew and understood the teachings of the Apostles. While Philemon's church had been active so long it hadn't gone through the steps that were now firmly established as necessary to keep the Body of Christ pure, it was a church that was known as being filled with and led by the Holy Spirit. Philemon, while unnamed as official pastor, had served in that capacity for many years.

But while Apollonia prepared for an addition to her family, sewing baby clothing, readying diapers and swaddling bands, and Onesimus busied himself building a cradle to hold his precious treasure, Philemon began hearing news that set his teeth on edge.

It began one day in the middle of the summer season. The new crop of olives was bursting to life in the groves and all the bookwork was complete thanks to Quintin's diligence, so Philemon was having a day of productive rest with his whole family gathered around on their home's front porch. Apphia, Quintin, Quintin's soon to be bride, Quinta, and Blandina all were there. Apphia was doing some much-needed mending, Quintin and Quinta were busily making moon eyes at each other. Blandina was making a rag doll for the baby who was soon-to-arrive in the little cottage across the olive grove and Philemon was using his awl and needle to stitch a sandal's straps to its insole. For some reason he had decided he wanted to try his hand at creating a pair of sandals. Usually, he simply purchased sandals, but he thought he had watched enough sandals being made that he wanted to try it himself. Whether the sandals turned out wearable or not, he could at least say he had tried his hand at it . . . and, so far, it looked like he might actually gain a pair of sandals from his efforts!

The conversation meandered across many topics and was currently centered on Apollonia's recent decision to remove herself from the public eye and remain sequestered at home to await the arrival of the baby. She had made it thus far, but the nearer to term she was the more danger she was in to lose the baby. Everyone knew that if she were startled by a loud noise or stretched her arms too far above her head or lifted something too heavy or even shouted too loudly, she could miscarry or have a still birth!

"Well," Apphia was saying, "I remember one day while I was carrying Blandina I slipped and fell on the floor and couldn't rise to my feet. I could see the whole day stretching before me because I knew you were in the groves and we didn't have the workers we do now. I got so desperate I shouted as loudly as possible for you . . . I was so afraid, but I knew that staying on the floor until you came home was just not possible . . . I have to wonder whether all these things the physicians tell us are really true . . . but I think Apollonia is wise to . . ."

A courier riding a golden horse with a white mane and tail turned into their yard and made directly for the group. Dismounting

from his palomino he removed a scroll from his bags and hurried to
Philemon's side.

"Begging your pardon, Sir, but I have a message from Mistress
Philomena of Ephesus to someone named Onesimus . . . would
you be he?"

"No. Onesimus lives across the olive grove in the cottage you can see
from here. He will be glad to hear from his friend," Philemon replied.

The rider shook his head as if he disagreed with this statement. "I'm
afraid not. There is trouble brewing and the Mistress is calling for help."
With this announcement, the messenger stooped down and drew a
curved line in the dirt path.

Frowning slightly, Philemon laid aside his work and stepped down
to the path where he bent down and drew the completing curved line,
to create a fish. "Go now," he murmured. "And we will pray that God go
with you."

The man remounted his steed and turned to make his way through
the olive grove to the home of Onesimus.

"Thank you so much, Donatilla, for staying here with Apollonia until
the child comes," Onesimus said for what seemed the hundredth time.
"I don't know what I would do if you weren't able to do this for me."

Donatilla patted his hand and made soothing noises. "We are all
part of the Body of Christ and need to help one another when we can,"
she said quietly. "Besides, what would I do at home with Epimachus off
with you on your great rescue? The children are grown and gone and
I would just rattle around with no one to take care of!"

Onesimus gave his very pregnant wife one last hug and kiss and
started for the door as Donatilla spoke again, "Babies come when they
come and I've seen enough of them into this world so that you can rest
easy, Onesimus! You go meet your friend on the road and bring her back
here to safety. We will be just fine."

One last worried glance at his sweetheart and he mounted Poppy,
nodded at his companion Epimachus, and wheeled his mount toward
the road. They were headed out to meet Philomena somewhere along the
road from Ephesus where she would be traveling toward him and a safe

place to hide from the persecutions that had spread beyond Rome and were now stirring up the citizens of Greece.

The minute they were out of sight, a low groan escaped Apollonia's white lips.

Donatilla looked over at her sweaty brow and the tightened skin around her eyes and mouth and nodded. "You did well to hide it as you did. He would never have gone had he known how close you are!" She took the mother-to-be by the waist and led her to her bed. "You make yourself as comfortable as possible and I will get the water started and go tell Apphia that she will soon want to be here to greet her adopted grandson!"

Apollonia nodded silently and lay down on her side, with her back to the wall and her knees drawn up as high as she could get them as Donatilla set to work.

αω

CHAPTER TWENTY-NINE

hat a fanciful tale!" Epimachus exclaimed. "A runaway slave passes through a town just in time to witness the beating and branding of another runaway slave? What an amazing imagination you have!"

Onesimus smiled and shook his head. "It isn't my imagination, friend Epimachus. It is a part of my life. I know that you had not yet heard the Gospel at that time, but I was the runaway slave that saw that fearsome sight. I was so angry and bitter . . . so filled with fear that the Master I served would treat me as my family had always treated accused slaves in our household that, to me, there was no alternative I could see."

"And who was your master, friend. And why aren't you a slave now? Were you a bond slave?" He said it with a slight touch of sarcasm in his voice. He knew Onesimus well enough that he understood he would never lie . . . but he also knew Onesimus well enough that he understood what a great storyteller he was!

"My Master was Philemon, the man for whom I now work. I was a plain and simple slave-market slave, bought and sold," he said this without a trace of the old bitterness. "My father came upon hard financial times and sold me into slavery to pay his debts." He continued to speak, "Philemon came to the slave market to purchase a slave that was able to do book-work for him. When the slaver told him about how strong this one was and how agile this one was my heart was pounding because I knew I could do what he was asking. Philemon was getting so irritated

at this bounder who kept trying to sell him half-starved field workers.
he turned to me (the only one the slaver hadn't gotten to) and said, "Do
you speak relatively fluent Greek?"

I nodded and answered him yes.

Then he said, "How much is 25 amphora of olive oil going to
sell for?"

I was taken aback but answered as best I could, "I haven't any
idea what it would sell for right now, but if you will give me a cost per
amphora I will gladly give you the answer."

Philemon slapped his hand down on my shoulder and told the
slaver, "This one! I told you I wanted someone with a brain, not a lot of
muscle . . . although it looks as though you have half-starved the muscle
off of your field-hands!"

The slaver, of course, protested his kindly treatment of us but
Philemon turned to me, "How has he treated you? Did you eat regularly?
How many times a day?"

"I didn't want to make things worse for the remaining slaves, but
I had to be honest with my new master, so I told him we were fed once
a day. It was then I knew I had cast the winning lot for he turned to the
slaver and grabbed the front of his toga. He pulled him so close their
noses were touching and said, 'I may come back next week for another
worker . . . I do not want to hear the same thing I was just told! You will
feed them at least twice a day and it had better be eatable food, not the
slop I've no doubt you have been giving them. I may not be back until
the new moon, but I had better find you *still* feeding these humans as
if they were human!' After negotiations and payment were complete,
he took the chains from my wrists and told me to follow him. I was so
grateful to him. It never entered my head that I could get lost within the
crowds of Colossae. So, I followed him home and he talked to me along
the way as if I mattered! He told me what my duties would be, bought a
loaf of bread and gave me half of it. He treated me with the respect I had
never shown *our* slaves."

"Were you then a follower of The Way?"

Onesimus shook his head. "I had heard vague stories about this new
cult but had never been around anyone who followed Yeshua. When
I found out my new master held 'cult meetings' in his home every
week I was shocked. I wondered if they would sacrifice babies as I had

heard they did . . . I wondered if they would eat the flesh of someone as I had also heard. I was told I had to attend the meetings and I was very concerned . . . especially when there was no food provided on Lord's Day morning . . . I thought I was either going to be expected to eat a human or was going to have to fast all day!" he laughed.

"It must have seemed very strange to you. I know it did to me the first time I came into a meeting.

"How did you come to that time," Epimachus asked, "when you finally took to your heels and ran . . . if it's not too personal for me to ask."

So the conversation went, a pleasant time of talk and laughter as their mounts trotted along together, coming closer and closer to their meeting with the brave Philomena.

It didn't seem long at all before the two men were passing through the village where the branding had taken place.

Onesimus reached over and patted Epimachus' thigh. "This is it. This is where I saw the slave beaten and branded."

"It seems like such an ordinary town!" Epimachus observed, looking around at the streets with their donkeys and horses and people on foot going about their everyday business. "Only a slave's master is supposed to choose how to punish a runaway and yet these people took it on themselves to do so!" He shook his head in amazement.

"Well, I don't know. The master could have been among those who were there that day, but I don't think so. I believe the people just wanted some excitement," he shrugged. "I wish I knew where . . ." his words were cut off by a shout.

"Onesimus! How wonderful! I am so glad to see you!"

"Philomena! I was hoping you were bringing your family with you," Onesimus replied as the two jumped from their horses and embraced warmly. Onesimus grinned as Philomena's hair tip-tilted to the side as was its wont and he reached up and gave it a gentle shove back into place.

"Philomena, this is my friend and brother, Epimachus. Epimachus, this is the brave lady whose home was burned to the ground because of her faith, Philomena."

Epimachus gave a small salute from his horseback and Philomena smiled pleasantly at him. "We really need to keep moving, Onesimus.

I hope you weren't in need of a rest because there are brigands on our heels who would like nothing better than to find us on the road after dark."

"No. That's fine, my sister. We will have to find a place to camp tonight but, with your footman to help we will be able to keep watch through the night," and with that the two friends re-mounted their horses, turned them back the way the men had come, and traveled out of the village and back toward Onesimus' home.

The sun had only traveled a hand's breadth across the sky on the day Onesimus had departed when Apollonia moved from the bed to the birthing chair and, by sunset, a very tired but joyful woman was back in bed, with a brand-new baby boy at her breast. Apphia rushed home to tell Philemon and to send the slaves into the groves to collect olive branches and to use those branches to decorate the windows, doors, and doorstep of the little cottage to announce the birth of a son.

Having no knowledge that he was now a father, Onesimus found the camp site he had used on his journey back to Philemon's home from Rome. It was the same place he had been awakened in the night by a wild boar. While he hoped that in the years since Mr. Pig had found a new place to root for his dinner, he knew the little traveling party was in more danger from the foolish men who burned down Philomena's house and were still on her trail as she tried to make her way to safety than from any wild animals. The site itself was just a short way from the road, surrounded by bramble bushes on three sides and invisible from the road because of a large outcropping of rock that, from the road, looked as if it were impregnable. Indeed, the only reason Onesimus knew of this grove's existence was because he had stumbled upon it on his return trip from Rome.

Onesimus slept through the first watch and then rose to take his turn at guard duty. The footman, Adalbert, who had been footman to Philomena's father, would take third watch, which Onesimus would take care to ensure was a short one. At his age, Adalbert needed his sleep unbroken.

It was shortly after he had taken the watch that Onesimus was stirred to action by the sound of horse's hooves on the road beyond the rocks. Carefully, the watcher moved toward the boulder that stood eight feet high from the road but only five feet from the floor of the camp. Dropping to his knees, Onesimus crept forward until he could look down upon the road undetected. Two men were alighting from their saddles and discussing what should be done about "that cursed woman who defied the Emperor and all the gods."

"Well, I think we just need to find a place to rest tonight and we can take up the chase in the morning." The short, muscular man was already leading his horse to the opposite side of the road where there was a flat enough spot to graze the horses and bed down for what remained of the night. "Those two old vultures must be pretty tired by now! It won't be long and they will come walking up to us, 'O please, Mr. Carpophorus! Please take us to the nearest temple so we can burn incense to the true god, our emperor!' and *of course* we will gladly take them under our wing—*and run them through where they stand!*"

The taller man who looked to be made all of long, slender bones laughed and tugged his horse into the camp site but said not a word.

Onesimus took advantage of the noises made by the unsaddling of the horses and their staking out to worm his way back into his encampment. He found a small boulder to sit on and sat there mulling over what should be done. Should he awaken the camp and move out immediately…or after they heard snoring from across the way? Or should he surprise the thugs while they slept and…he couldn't even finish that thought although he carried his short sword in his tunic. Then he suddenly realized exactly what he needed to do and he nodded his head and quietly he moved from Epimachus to Philomena to Adalbert. Placing his left hand firmly over their mouths and holding his right finger to his lips, he awakened each one and whispered, "We will be staying right here in the morning. The pursuers have just bedded down across the road. They will start out again at first light and *we* will remain here long enough to break our fast. Then *we* will follow *them!*"

Onesimus knew it wouldn't have worked if the recent rain hadn't packed down the dirt of the road and made it almost as hard as rock. As it was, the hooves of the horses made not a dent in the road, so there was no trail to follow. Further down the road there was a fork where the pursuers would have to make a choice about which to take. Without any knowledge of where Philomena was headed or that she had any friends in the district, the choice would probably be to take the road toward Lystra where the trackers would assume Philomena would go to be lost in the crowds of strangers. Beyond that, Onesimus reflected, God would surely put those thoughts on them so they would choose the wrong path!

Onesimus kept watch until the pre-dawn light when he awoke Adalbert to take the watch for the rest of the night. He warned Adalbert to stay back away from the bluff so he couldn't be seen or heard from the road, and suggested he just find a comfortable place to sit and listen for any intruders. Then, Onesimus lay down and feigned sleep, but actually maintained a vigilant watchfulness. Adalbert was a fine footman for Philomena, but he was too old to handle some of the physical emergencies which might suddenly arise.

The noises of breaking camp and moving out drifted across the road and stirred the sleepers behind the rocks. Quietly moving around the camp, they listened intently as their pursuers discussed possible outcomes and moved onto the road. It wasn't long before they found themselves alone again in the peace of the morning and began to break fast and talk among themselves about a variety of subjects. About an hour later Onesimus began saddling up and they prepared to move on.

As they traveled up the road toward safety, Onesimus explained, "There really isn't much reason to hurry. We shall arrive at Philemon's house in time for the mid-day meal. If it hadn't been for those single-minded men, we would have been able to be there by mid-morning. Philomena, if you don't mind my asking, why are these men so *determined* to chase you down?"

Philomena spoke quietly, "I'm not certain why, but I know what I believe to be true. I met a group of five young girls in downtown Ephesus and became their friend. It was obvious from the first time I saw them that they were caught up in some form of prostitution, but I sensed that Yeshua wanted me to be their friend. Soon we were meeting weekly and I was telling them about Yeshua. One by one these girls came to accept that Yeshua was the one true God and, as they did so, they left their old life behind and moved into my home. I believe these men were their owners in their previous lives and would punish me for "taking *their* girls away." They burned down my house hoping that would make the girls return to them, but instead it just made them determined to defy these men. The girls teamed together and boarded a ship bound for Alexandria . . . I believe it was . . . Yes! It was called The *Swan*! The Master of the ship took them on, promising their safety when he heard what they were running from. It was when he drew the first half of the fish on the dock, though, that we knew he could be trusted!

Onesimus shook his head in amazement as unshed tears sprang to his eyes. The *Swan* was the very ship that had taken him to Rome and that, later, brought him back to Ephesus. On the second trip, Captain Alban had listened to all that Onesimus said concerning Yeshua and though Alban didn't announce his conversion at that time, it was obvious that he had later accepted the truth of what Onesimus had said. It was certainly as the Psalmist said, that God's message would never return without success!

αω

CHAPTER THIRTY

H ere we are!" Onesimus nearly crowed as he turned Poppy off the road and led the brave little band of refugees toward the sparkling white house.

He could hear murmurs arising from Philomena and Adalbert and he smiled inside as he realized what a stunning impression this property made on those who had never seen it before. But the inner smile soon grew to be a huge grin, then a war-whoop as he glanced across the olive groves and saw his own little cottage draped and swathed in olive branches.

He was a father! And it was a boy!

Without a word of explanation (although none was really needed after the two visitors saw the customary drapings on the cottage) and Onesimus spurred Poppy to a fast trot since she was simply too tired for a full-out gallop. Seconds later, Onesimus remembered his guests and shouted over his shoulder, "Eimai pateras!" (I'm a father!)

The visitors sat staring at each other, wondering what they should do until a muscular man approached them from the olive press saying, "You must be Philomena! I am Philemon, Onesimus's erstwhile master and now employer. Welcome to our home! We have heard what happened to you and you are more than welcome to abide with us as long as you require."

After helping the aged Adalbert and Philomena dismount, he brought them into his home.

"As you can see, Onesimus' homecoming was more of a surprise to him than he expected! In fact, Apollonia actually gave birth to their son just hours after his departure to rescue you! The naming ceremony will be this coming Lord's Day. It is nearly time for the mid-day meal and I would ask you to partake with us. We will leave the new parents to wonder over their new child and later on we will go for a visit when they have had a chance to be alone for a while, if that is suitable for you."

Both of the guests nodded as they seated themselves at the dining table and soon the sounds of grateful praise for provisions and for safety rose into the air as their weariness lifted in response to the loving welcome they had received.

"He's the most beautiful boy the Lord has ever made! Apple, you and this child are my whole world!" Onesimus whispered in love and wonder.

Apollonia smiled at the nickname Onesimus hadn't used since their marriage. He would tease her by calling her Apple as they walked through the olive groves or broke fast together on Sunday mornings. She pretended to be offended by the sobriquet but really thought it sweet of him to think of it, but the nickname had disappeared from his vocabulary shortly after their marriage, although neither of them realized it until this day.

She laughed as the child began to whimper in Onesimus' arms and he, in turn, looked so alarmed you would have thought he was being threatened by a bear. The new father quickly bent down and placed the baby in the arms of his mother and backed away, "I don't know what I did! Why is he crying? Did I do something wrong?" The panicked questions flew from Onesimus' mouth until Apollonia placed the baby at her breast and giggled at the fear in her husband's face.

"Husband, you did nothing to make him cry! He's a baby and will cry whenever he needs anything. He's hungry just now. Next time he may need to have a diaper change, or he might be sleepy and need to be held until he sleeps," Apollonia explained.

Onesimus nodded sheepishly and replied, "I think I shall leave the care of the child in your capable hands, dearest. Men have no abilities to care for babies." He turned and paced across the room to the front door where he proclaimed (with a touch of pomposity), "Babies are women's work. I shall leave him to your care until he can communicate his needs with words!"

Gales of laughter from Apollonia surprised Onesimus and made the baby lose his concentration on eating and stare up at his mother. "Oh! Onesimus! You are so funny! You will soon understand that whoever is closest to baby when he cries will be expected, by both him and me, to pick him up and help him. Don't worry, it will become a natural reaction soon enough."

Onesimus stood blinking at her until he, too, began to laugh. "Of course! I certainly sounded as if I could be a senator, didn't I? What a pretentious speech! I think what I was really trying to say was that I will let you teach me how to answer his needs and we . . . *together* . . . will take care of him!"

After the meeting on the Lord's Day, Philomena and Adalbert watched as Onesimus and Apollonia holding the baby walked to the center of the group of Christian brothers and sisters who had gathered to worship the God of the universe and to hear for the first time, the name of the new child born this week. While the naming ceremony had been a part of Greek life for as long as anyone could remember, this naming custom would introduce a different ritual than those of the pagan past.

Holding their newborn child, parents would stand before the church to declare the child's name . . . and that time was now upon them.

"My dear friends, brothers, and sisters," Philemon began. "Come now Onesimus, Apollonia, and the gift God has given them to cherish to speak the child's name. Onesimus, would you now speak?"

Onesimus took the child from Apollonia and whispered his name in his ear. Whether the breath of the whisperer tickled or the child approved of the name, for some reason the baby smiled and all the women present ahhed and hmmmed in admiration. Then Onesimus raised the boy above his head and prayed, "Father, we give this child, this gift from you, back to you and pledge to raise him in the knowledge of your word." Lowering the child again he handed the baby to Philemon who leaned him up against his chest in a sitting position so that the congregation could see him.

Apollonia stepped forward. Her voice was louder than anyone had ever suspected she could speak but it still carried a softness of spirit in it. "In memory of the man who brought the good news to Onesimus, and in gratitude for the man who has been like a father to us both, the child is named Paulus Philemon."

The congregation gasped and began to murmur. Philemon almost dropped the baby in his shock. Onesimus stood there and grinned. Apollonia smiled with glee, and Apphia, Philemon's wife, beamed forth her delight. Naming the child after Philemon would have been a social gaff for that name was reserved for the eldest son's first son . . . but naming the child after Paulus and leaving Philemon for his secondary name was a wonderful honor.

CHAPTER THIRTY-ONE

P hilemon sat at his desk in the olive press and stared at the missive in front of him. His brow looked as if someone had wadded up a piece of parchment and his eyes held a sadness that only time would be able to remove.

How can I tell him? What could I possibly say? Onesimus' whole family gone! Father, Mother both commanded to burn incense to Caesar and refusing, paying for their faithfulness to God with their lives. At least it wasn't in the arena or as a human torch, Philemon thought with a sigh. *Just beheaded.* He rolled his eyes at the phrase *"just beheaded"* . . . *that's all* . . . *"just beheaded!"*

Protos, as well. His eyes traveled back to the letter which had been sent here from the body of Christ in Colossae where Onesimus' family had worshipped. He read on, *"It is with great sorrow I ask you to convey our grief to our dear brother, Onesimus. Protos also refused to bow to Caesar's soldiers and paid with his life. Unlike his parents, his was not an easy death. He was dragged through the streets while tied to a Centurion's horse.* Philemon closed his eyes against the words and wondered how much he should convey to Onesimus . . . perhaps he could skim over the uglier parts.

He shook his head without thought. *Not Onesimus. He would demand to know the details. I will start with the basics and let him ask questions,* Philemon thought. *He will have to drag the particulars out of me!* He determined.

To help with the horrible task ahead, he went to the house and called on Philomena and Adalbert to go with him to help break the news.

It was a subdued group of friends that trekked through the olive groves to the small cottage and called out, "Ho! The house!" It wasn't a very loud call, considering there was a small child within that could very well be napping, but it was loud enough to bring Onesimus to the door.

"Ah! My best friends! What brings you to our door this day?" he asked with a smile.

The company simply stood there, uncomfortable and unspeaking, trying to find the right approach to this news.

As the silence continued, Onesimus' smile faded and concern shined from his eyes. "What is it? Why come you?"

Philemon stepped forward, "Onesimus, my friend. We've news to bring and it is not happy news, I'm afraid. Can we sit?"

At Onesimus' nod, the four people made their way to the hip-high stoop and seated themselves in a row along the front. With no discussion, they arranged themselves around Onesimus who stood leaning against the stoop in the middle. Their positioning an unconscious display of support with Philemon on Onesimus' right, Philomena on his left and Adalbert beside Philomena.

As Philemon opened his mouth to speak, Apollonia stepped through the door, "Oh! Hello! I've just gotten Little Paulus to sleep. How nice to see you all!" She stepped off the stoop and tried to seat herself beside Adalbert, but he moved over, as did Philomena, so she ended up next to Onesimus. Adalbert shifted around to sit beside Philemon.

By this time, Onesimus was beginning to frown with concern. All this dancing for position and Philemon's mention that it was not happy news, made his heart begin to pound and he suddenly realized he was holding his breath when his lungs began to ache.

"What?!" he cried out. "What is it you must tell me?"

Philemon laid his large paw on Onesimus' shoulder and began again.

"Today I have had a letter concerning your father . . . and mother . . . and Protos."

Onesimus reached blindly for Apollonia's hand.

"The shepherd of the body of Christ at Colossae wrote to let you know that . . . your family—all of them—are now in the arms of Yeshua."

The hearer jumped to his feet and shouted, "NO! What do you mean? Speak it plainly, sir! I cannot bear this slow revelation! Tell me quickly for I cannot abide the waiting!"

Philemon rose to stand in front of Onesimus and took him by the shoulders.

"Your father and mother were called upon to burn incense to Caesar and when they refused, they were immediately beheaded. Protos, as well, lost his life rather than bow down."

Onesimus' gaze intensified as he stared at his mentor. "And how was his life taken from him? Since you speak of him separately, I must believe his d... his d... that he was treated differently."

Philemon made an on-the-spot decision to pull no punches. It would do no good since Onesimus was Onesimus. "Upon his third refusal before the body of Christ to burn incense to the Emperor, he was tied to a Centurion's horse and dragged through the streets until he was no longer . . . in his flesh."

Onesimus' knees gave way and before anyone could grab him, he was sitting in the dirt of the yard, shaking and weeping.

Apollonia and Philemon both joined him in the dirt while Philomena and Adalbert (whose bones were too frail to ever rise from the dirt) sat on the stoop with their arms around each other. All wept together as the pain and grief washed over their beloved friend.

CHAPTER THIRTY-TWO

K eeping his eyes closed, Onesimus stretched out his hand to the cold hollow on the other side of the bed. He sniffed the air—nothing cooking. Still with closed eyes he tilted his head to the side and listened closely—there! Just a little bit of a *ssshhh*ing sound of small feet slipping across the floor and gurgles emanating from nearby. He rolled over to face the room instead of the wall. Slowly, reluctantly, he opened his eyes—first just a slit so he was peering through his own lashes, where he saw the blurry outline of a feminine form, then slowly opening them a little more and a little more until they were open and seeing the precious vision of a woman with her child at her breast.

"Onesimus! I've called you twice!" Apollonia cried. "It's Lord's Day! Time to arise and give glory to the God of the Universe!"

The sleepy one smiled as he realized his beloved wife was using part of the same phrase Justin, the chief houseman, shouted every Lord's Day morning to rouse the sleeping slaves. Slave or no, the phrase brought back fond memories of those first days, when he wondered why there was no food to break the fast with on his first Lord's Day morning . . . his fear that he would be required to fast all day or eat human babies . . . until he saw the people coming to the house with basket after basket of delicious food . . . and not a roasted baby among them!

As he washed and dressed, he watched his beloved pack their Lord's Day basket with apples baked on the hearth with honey and nuts; figs and raisins; and roasted eggs . . . but no olives. Never olives. He had asked her about the lack of olives in her basket soon after they were married and she replied, "God asks our best as a sacrifice. Olives are plentiful and free for us and it is no sacrifice to supply what God has given freely."

While Onesimus wasn't sure he agreed with her philosophy he wasn't going to question her heart or challenge her thought processes by demanding that olives be included. He simply smiled to himself, slipped his feet into his sandals, and took hold of the basket to carry it to the meeting as Apollonia walked beside him with Little Paulus.

The following hour was filled with greetings of brothers and sisters in the Lord, laughter and discussion with former slaves and current slaves of Philemon, breaking fast with friends and celebrating the Lord's Supper with fellow believers. It seemed only a short span before Philemon was calling for everyone to find seats and join with others in the praise and worship of the most high God.

As the prayers and praises lifted to God Onesimus felt his heart lifted as well. In the midst of the worship a woman stood up and began to speak. "One here has been asking the Lord for confirmation that he is calling for you to make a big change in your life. He says to you, 'You need not fear. I have chosen you. I will go with you. I am calling you and tomorrow you must reveal your answer to those who must know. The need is great and you are called to help fulfill that need.'"

Apollonia reached for Onesimus' hand and looked into his eyes. His heart was pounding and his hands were shaking. He knew this was a Word of Knowledge just for him and Apollonia, who smiled widely and nodded her head, her eyes shining and excited for she knew as well, that their new adventure was about to begin.

CHAPTER THIRTY-THREE

S o, you are sure that Quintin is ready to ride that horse alone?"
Philemon asked. A small vertical crease had appeared between
his brows as he thought of his son being responsible for all the
business accounts. The boy was, after all, only fifteen. He closed his eyes
and shook his head, *Listen to me!* He thought ruefully, *"only" fifteen! At
his age I was preparing to marry Apphia and had already taken over the
reins of the business from Father and Father wasn't able to help me when
I got into trouble as I shall be for Quintin, either!* His mind veered away
from contemplating his father's moon-madness that had come upon him
when he was only 35 years old! Those were bad times . . . ugly times and
he didn't enjoy the contemplation of them.

Onesimus sat silently as he watched Philemon's face display a wide
range of emotions, from pride in his son to worry and sadness. While
Onesimus didn't know for a certainty what had brought the latter to his
employer's face, he knew enough to allow a space of time before speaking
again but Philemon beat him to the first word.

"What are your plans now that Quintin will take over the rest of
your duties?"

Tilting his head, Onesimus cleared his throat and began to speak.
"Well, I really didn't want to leave you—ever—you have been so kind to
me and Apollonia! But I feel I was given a great gift when I was allowed
to study under Paulus for two years and that gift isn't being used as God
would want it used.

"There are so many places where Christians need sound doctrine
and while the Holy Spirit abides with them, physically they have only
the Apostles' letters they have managed to collect. Sometimes false

teachers come in among them and lead them astray and my heart is burdened for them.

"The teaching ministry of Lystra went well and Perfectus of Lystra has taken the leadership of that body upon himself. So did Laodicea's catechisms do well. Epaphras has taken up the pastoring of them and Nympha guides them when Epaphras is busy in Hieropolis so those churches are covered but there are so many in need of guidance and God has been sending me dreams of these brothers and sisters calling me to teach them and to guide those who have no shepherd. So many of our own have been taken and martyred that many of the churches have lost their leaders and I fear for their well-being. What I really would like to do is to teach the teachers! To gather those who lead the churches and help them . . ."

Philemon held up his hand to halt the flow of words spilling from Onesimus' lips. "You need not convince me. I have known for some time that you and Apollonia were going to leave me to follow Yeshua's calling! I was just waiting until you were free of your bookkeeping duties . . ." his voice trailed off and his glance entered the far distance. "Why do you think I suggested you teach Quintin my bookkeeping method?" He smiled and continued, "You know Quintin is preparing to marry Quinta after this harvest? That new construction I have been supervising for the last year just across the meadow from the house will be Quintin and Quinta's home . . . but of course you knew that since you were the one ordering the supplies to build it. Construction is almost done now and you are more than welcome to remain in the cottage as long as you need it."

Onesimus shook his head, "That will only be necessary for one month since the brothers at Lystra have prepared a home for us. Since Lystra is so central, traveling and teaching from there should be the wisest method to reach the most people. I thought we would put Quintin into his new position as 'official bookkeeper' but we would stay here for one more month. During that month Apollonia will finish training someone in her kitchen duties and, if Quintin has any trouble I would be nearby to help. Would that work for you?"

Philemon stood and took Onesimus by the shoulders. "I shall miss you my friend, but I know God has more than bookkeeping in his plans for you!"

It seemed as if both men had something in their eyes since they were both blinking rapidly. And thus, Quintin became Philemon's right-hand man . . . the position Onesimus had held for several years . . . and Onesimus stepped into the very large sandals that Paulus had left behind when he stepped onto the golden streets and ran to meet his Savior.

αω

AUTHOR'S NOTE:
Although *Slave to Grace* was taken from the book of Philemon, it is a little difficult to pull enough fiction from a single chapter to create a second book! So while this novel is based on its predecessor, *Slave to Grace,* and seeks to follow Onesimus' further exploits, it is impossible to call this book a "Bible story"—and I really wouldn't want to. What I can say is that, even though it is NOT a Bible story, it IS true to the times about which I write. The Gospel was being spread and was beginning to come up against the strong opposition of the mighty Roman Empire.